PR[illegible]

Tu[illegible]

- 'Another gripping story . . . good stuff from an author who never disappoints' – *Independent*
- 'A raw and perceptive story' – *Books for Keeps*

Firestarter

- 'A gripping and edgy thriller that keeps the reader on the edge of their seat' – *Bookseller*
- 'Catherine Forde's novels have the emotional impact of a clenched fist to the stomach. She writes powerful prose that deliver firm blows' – *Achuka*

The Drowning Pond

- 'Bitingly plausible . . . a gripping page-turner' – *Guardian*
- 'Expertly crafted, with characters full of bite and vitality' – *Glasgow Herald*

Skarrs

- 'A novel that is both troubling and inspirational' – *Guardian*
- 'A heady mix of broken glass emotions, tough, edgy dialogue and page-turning storytelling' – *Publishing News*

Fat Boy Swim

- 'Fat Boy Swim should be force-fed [illegible]ery secondary school child[illegible]
- 'Powerful, [illegible]nny' – *The Times*
- 'A moving, [illegible], roller-coaster, acid-etched story' – *Bookseller*

Also by Catherine Forde

Dead Men Don't Talk
Bad Wedding
Exit Oz
Firestarter
I See You Baby . . . (with Kevin Brooks)
L-L-L-LOSER
Skarrs
Sugarcoated
The Drowning Pond
The Finding
Think Me Back
Tug of War

PLAYS
Empty
The Sunday Lesson

To Fraserburgh Academy

Fifteen Minute Bob

Catherine FORDE

Cathy Forde

EGMONT

EGMONT
We bring stories to life

First published in Great Britain 2010
by Egmont UK Limited
239 Kensington High Street
London W8 6SA

The characters and situations depicted in this work of fiction are entirely products of the author's imagination.

ISBN 978 1 4052 2930 2

1 3 5 7 9 10 8 6 4 2

www.egmont.co.uk
www.catherineforde.co.uk

A CIP catalogue record for this title is available from the British Library

Typeset by Avon DataSet Ltd, Bidford on Avon B50 4JH
Printed and bound in Great Britain by the CPI Group

For Frances and Andy with fond thanks

CONTENTS

ACT 1, SCENE ONE

Imagine this, okay?:

It's your Sixth Form Parents' Night. And here's this bloke dandering towards you. He's dressed in velvet coat-tails and leather trousers. There's a top hat on his head, insane pointy boots on his feet. He's twirling a cane. And staring at you through black eyeliner . . . Or should that be guyliner? I wouldn't know.

Below a scrappy moustache – looks feathered on with the same pencil he used round his eyes – this bloke's mouth is wide. Moving constantly. Like he's babbling to himself.

Now. What would you think if you saw this guy heading in your direction?

Maybe: *Check OUT this weirdo?*

Please don't let him come and talk to ***me****.*

Snap.

*

*Oh, boy. Not tonight. Just go a-**way***, I'm cringing while I track this lone pedestrian weaving among the cars trying to park in our schoolyard.

I watch him swaying. Threshing his cane from left to right to mow a pathway for himself. Ignoring warning toots. The hand-gestures of swerving drivers. Even big-shot drivers like my best mate Barry Masterton's dad. There Mr Masterton is, making slick work reversing his latest Merc into a tight space, steering her like some sugar-daddy waltzing a full-spec supermodel round a ballroom. Till Mr Guyliner cuts behind, forcing an *eek!* of panic from the Merc's brakes. No wonder Mr Masterton zeeps his window. He's mouthing words that send his missus lunging across the dashboard to muzzle his gob.

Meanwhile, Mr Guyliner's unaware he's pushing Mr M to the brink of embolism. Oblivious, he is. To the hissed exchange ping-ponging across the bonnet of Mr M's Merc now: '*Sweetheart, calm down. You know it's not the poor boy's fault that man is . . .*'

Or to the double-takes he earns from every other parent arriving.

Mr Guyliner is far too caught up with . . . I was

going to say 'singing', but he's more kind of *chanting*. Rapping, even. With a spot of beat-boxing thrown in for good measure.

All at me:

'Hey Mista Perfect, check ya standin' there:
Uptight in your neat clothes and combed down hair.
Doin' what's expected. Keepin' to de plan.
Stickin' to de pathway. Working for De Man.
Oooooh laa laaa. Oooooh laa laaaa . . .
Always stickin' to de pathway. Workin' for De Man . . .'

As I'm being serenaded, Mr Guyliner taps his cane against my collarbone in time to the rhythm of his words. It's not painful. Just annoying. Extremely. Meantime, his free hand roots in his jacket pocket.

A couple of dads hesitate. One's Annette Muir's. I recall him from the day I tour-guided him and Annette round St Bernard's before she enrolled for Sixth Form. Don't ask me how I recognise him, though. From the instant we met, it was only his girl my eyes were glued to. Treacle-black hair Annette has. The prettiest smile. Happens to be in two of my A-level classes now, so I see a lot of her. And we're kind of . . . I don't know . . . something . . . *unsaid* to each other, I suppose. Something waiting to happen. Maybe . . . We have been ever since Annette's first day when our thoughtless School Chaplain had her squirming in front of the whole year during Pastoral Support when she didn't know a bloody soul.

'Do tell what brings you across the city to *this* school,' old Father No-Wits beckoned her to stand and inform everyone. 'Too much trouble for the nuns, were we?'

'I'd to come here because my mum and dad have just divorced and I've moved house. I loved my old school,' Annette mumbled as she sank into the seat beside me. Then I heard her gulp and sniff.

'Hey, you'll be fine at St Bernard's. I'll make sure you're all right. I'm Rory, by the way,' I whispered. Kinda brave of me; uncharacteristically brave. But I just did.

Back to Parents' Night and here's Annette's old man returning the favour: 'Everything all right there, son?'

'I'm fine, thanks, Mr Muir,' I lie, relieved to note how the sensible majority of parents elect to quick-march past, pretending this scene at the school gates just isn't happening. Only my mate Smillie's dippy, 'I'm a neo-hippy' mum lingers. Half pouting at Mr Guyliner. Eyebrows arched. Until Smillie's dad tugs her floaty sleeve.

'Verity, come away,' he barks, leaving me and Mr Guyliner alone in the schoolyard.

Him blowing a mouth organ now.

In.

My.

Face.

2

COULD DO BETTER

Shit. I cannot be-*lieve* my dad has shown up. In thirteen years –*thirteen years* – he's *never* troubled Parents' Night. Never actually set foot in St Bernard's before. Not even when he was between jobs. Slobbing. Mum working double, sometimes triple shifts.

'You've *never* even picked me up when I've been sick. So why tonight?' I snap at Dad. My idiot dad. Mr Guyliner.

Lucky we're still in the schoolyard when I point these details out because Dad responds by ruffling my hair back into the natural pubic frizz I've inherited from him. And me after spending an hour gelling it flat and doing a parting for Parents' Night.

'Well observed, Einstein.'

'And where's Mum?' I hiss like a snake with a hangover. 'She *always* comes.'

Dad shrugs. Ripples up a scale on his mouth organ.

Back down. Playing for time.

'Thought,' he blow-mumbles, 'I'd cut my lady some slack. Mosey on over to check out the suits'n'beaks for myself. Do The *Daaad*, y'know?'

Knocking his knees together, Dad breaks into a body-pop routine. He combines it with The Twist.

'Do de Daaaad, man.' He flaps his elbows like a chicken who needs glucosamine, still Twisting as we follow all the other straightforward parents of his vintage into the school building.

'I'm also here,' he's wheezing a bit now, 'because some wise dude said you oughta do somethin' every day that scares you. Y'know Bob coulda said that: *Do somethin' every day that scares you.*'

Dad's lying, of course. Not about Bob, who you better believe I'll be coming to in due course. But about why he's here tonight.

And to think ten minutes ago I'd been feeling so pleased with myself.

Bet Mum'll be chuffed seeing me on Prefect duty at the gates, I'd been thinking. In my blazer. Lapels sagging gently under the weight of all my Merit badges:

Debating

Lunch Monitor

School Council

Computing

Photography

Academic Excellence

Science Club.

Normally, of course, and so you don't get the wrong idea about me, I only wear my Prefect badge. That's compulsory. But I thought I should sport the Full Monty tonight, mainly for Mum, though also to *showcase the respectable face of Sixth Form incarnate. Smart, hardworking, heading for university and a glittering future*.

By the way, those aren't my words. Just because I'm a Prefect doesn't mean I'm a tosser or a geek.

Headmaster Stanton gave me this guff while he steered me into Meet and Greet position. Brushed non-existent dandruff from my shoulders.

'Here's the drill, Rory. Firm handshake to every parent. Good eye contact, and –' Stanton was already striding off – 'steer your mater my way so I can report what a ne'er do well she's raising. Only joking! But she *is* coming?'

'Definitely, Sir.'

'So where *is* Mum? Is she all right, Dad?'

'*More* than all right. Because she's my righteous angel. Hey, lookee that painting.' Dad won't catch my eye. 'Rock formations, I'd say . . .'

Rock formations, my arse. We're in the science corridor now. Dad double making sure he can't deal with any more questions by scrutinising a blown-up photograph of decaying teeth. His mouth organ is clamped to his face.

'Is Mum working a double shift?' I persist over his raspy wheezing. 'Have you been sacked *again*?'

Dad pulls his shoulders up to his ears, confirming that my line of cross-examination is spot-on. Still squinting at the festering teeth, he hums harmony to a tune he's puffing on his mouth organ. When his foot stomps the floor and his eyes close, I know he's definitely bluesing me out for a reason.

'Dad!'

While Dad puffs harder, and I shout louder, Doctor Martin, my Physics teacher, peeks from his classroom.

'Gentlemen. Would you care to step . . .?' He interrupts his normally well-behaved science-sponge of a student –

me, that is – wrestling a mouth organ from a bloke tarted up like a fairground barker.

'Oh, dear me,' bleats Doc Martin just as I'm on the point of snapping Dad's cane across my knees. And growling into his painted face, 'Stop embarrassing me –'

'I embarrass YOU? Puh.' Dad's guff of indignation is whisky-tinged. 'Lookit you with your side-parting.' He draws an outline round me in the air. 'Cut loose, sunshine.'

When Dad flicks the tip of his cane at my hair and I raise my arm to fend him off, Doc Martin steps in to separate us. Unfortunately his face gets in the way. Though fortunately he's wearing his owly specs.

My crucial university referee could have lost an eye in the crossfire otherwise.

3
ALL MAPPED OUT

The only good thing about Parents' Night is its brevity.

Because twenty minutes after Dad cavorts into St Bernard's, he's sidestepping up the science corridor.

'Free at last, free at last, praise the Lord!' he proclaims, entertaining sumptious, scrumptious Selina Sutherland and her gaping parents with jazz hands and a dodgy Al Jolson impersonation.

'We's a-goin' home. Lawdy, lawdy! Faster'n the speed of light . . . Hey, Rory?'

Naturally, I'm scuffing well behind, pretending I have NO genetic link whatsoever to this limelight case. But when Dad reverse moonwalks to find out what's keeping me, my cover is blown.

'Ya listenin', Einstein?: *"Faster'n the speed of light."* Physics, yeah? Maybe your genius gene comes from ol'dada, after all. Anyway, we's a-splittin' dis Castle of Doom. *Ugh!* How can you stand that hairy ol' Maths witch day in day out? One of her eyes was going to the shops and the other was coming back –'

Headmaster Stanton, about to walk through the door Dad's pistoning in his face, definitely catches Dad's outburst, much of which concerns his wife, my hag of a Maths teacher. I don't linger to analyse his reaction. Just tuck my head down. Skulk after Dad all the way to the bus stop.

We have to sit upstairs so he can chain-smoke. And, yes, yes; I know it's my civic duty, but what's the point giving him The Speech about breaking the law, polluting the planet etc., etc.?

It's not like Dad'd *listen*. Not to me. He stopped paying any attention to me about twelve years ago. Soon as he sussed how I preferred number puzzles and Horrible Science to free music lessons and the smell of gatefold sleeves and vinyl. Anyway, now there's no audience to outrage, Dad's locked into himself, droning through the rollie clamped between his teeth. Stuff about 'having life all mapped out'.

Dad's voice is monotone. Just loud enough for our fellow passengers on the top-deck to cut him anxious *there's-a-loony-on-the-bus* looks. Since it's pointless asking him to pipe down, I close my eyes. Try to zone out. But what happens instead is inside my head a curtain rises. Three excruciating exchanges between me, Dad and my subject teachers replay in all their dramatic horror.

Physics:

Doctor Martin: *(returning his spectacle lens to its frame)* Oh dear me.

Blade, Rory's dad: Sorry I hit your goggles, friend. Accidento. Lucky I missed your eye, eh? Einstein here was horsin' about. Naughty-naughty in class too, is he?

Rory: *Dad . . .*

Doctor Martin: Oh, oh, now. I assure you, Rory *never* misbehaves, Mr Ryan. In fact - oh please sit, will you? - your s-s-son's the most diligent student I've . . . I've . . . in thirty-five years of . . . of . . . Yes. Truly g-g-g-gifted physicist. Intuitive, enquiring, industrious. In fact . . . R-R-Rory reminds me of myself as a young man . . .

PAUSE.

Blade: Well . . . ain't that f-f-fine? Everythin' all mapped out.

Rory: *Dad!*

Doctor Martin: Is . . . is there anything you wish to ask me, Mr R-R-Ryan?

Blade: Are we through?

Exit ***Blade***.

Exit ***Rory***.

*

Mathematics:

Mrs 'Stat' Stanton: You're late. Two minutes.

Rory: S-sorr . . .

Blade: Jeeeeeezo, keep the beard on lady!

Rory: *Dad!*

Mrs Stanton: I beg your pardon, Mr Ryan?

Blade: Said keep the beard on, lady. We getting invited into your parlour or what?

PAUSE.

Listen, if it's all the same, just gimme the

lowdown on Mr Perfect here. Means I'll be outa your life before you eat me all up -

Rory: *Dad!*

Mrs Stanton: I beg your pardon, Mr Ryan?

Blade: *(attempts sign language)* How. Is. The. Boyo. Doing?

Rory: *Daaaaad!!!!*

Mrs Stanton: Rory's progress is excellent. If you come over to this computer we can access his Personal Grade Progression Profile . . .

Blade: *(exiting)* All sounds tickety-boo. Rory, don't be keepin' daddio late for the next appointment now.

Rory: Sorry, Mrs Stanton. Bye, Mrs Stanton. Dad, wait up!

Blade: (off) What big teeth she had. A-whoooooohhhhh . . .

*

Chemistry:

Miss Sweet: Hiya, Rory. Dontcha look smart?

How you doing? This your dad? Hi-ya, Mr Ryan. Rory's just *fan*-tastic at Chemistry. My best ever pupil. Well, not that I've had many -

Blade: - It's Blade, sweetheart.

Miss Sweet: I'm Miss Sweet. Heather, I mean.

Blade: Sweet! Heather? Hey, cat I dig sings 'bout a Heather. '*Strawberry blonde with a dirty mind.*' Your hair's more honey, sweet-cheeks. Hey, and *you* teach my son by-o-lo-gy. No wonder he's a-keen on book-learnin', ma'am.

Rory: *Dad!*

(***Rory*** yanks ***Blade*** from ***Miss Sweet's*** room.)

Rory: (off) God's sake. Y'old sleazeball.

*

There you have some reasons why, despite a clutch of stonking reports, I sit next to Dad on the bus and I feel . . .

Well . . . crap.

And I should be elated. Proud, at least. I would be. If Mum was here.

'Keep it up there now, pet,' she'd pat my knee. Would slip me a five spot if she could manage it. But sitting next to Dad, beneath his grey veil of fag smoke, I just feel *low*. Weirdly, I now have these lyrics looping round and round in my head. And I'm not talking about those harmless ones Dad chanted about me being Mr Perfect at the school gates. These are *my* lyrics, this time. To a tune that isn't. Though it's one that's grown up with me. Been absorbed. Memorised, like a science formula, so I can't shake this particular tune away. Or the accusing, nasal voice that sings it.

Bob Blade's voice.

Though in my head I'm not singing his original lyrics to 'Wouldn't Bank on me, Sugar'. A song Bob Blade's been singing since 1963. The year my dad was born.

That's what's *really* annoying about this song I can't silence. I have NO interest in music, yet the lyrics by this 'cat' dad 'digs' to the point of idolatry, have rewritten themselves in *my* head. So now my gloomy version of Bob's bitter song soundtracks yet another stretch of time in Dad's company, taunting me – in Blade's voice – how 'I ain't never gonna make you proud, Dad, coz I'm the biggest let-down of your life'.

The pair of us sit like strangers on a journey, Dad turned ninety degrees from me, shoulders hunched, muttering through drags on his rollie.

I feel his disappointment in me pulsing the space between us like sonar.

While my head sings in Bob's voice.

4
BOBWASHED

Oooh! Bob has a lot to answer for.

Bob Blade, that is.

Heard of him?

If *you* haven't, your parents will have. Ask them. Ask your grandparents too. I'm not kidding. See, Bob was born way back in 1940. Plain Robert Alan Browning. In Sarnia, Ontario, Canada. Making records since 1962. You might even recognise some of his songs. He's written *hundreds*. Literally.

But no big deal if you don't know Blade from Adam. Or Bowie. Or Bruce. Or Brandon. Bob's an old-timer. I don't care if he's still making number one albums or out-there charity Christmas albums; he's an old-timer now.

So far as I'm concerned, it's not the end of the world if you've never shut your eyes. Opened your heart to Blade singing 'Ol' Blind Boy, Lucky Stone'.

Do that, according to Dad, and you experience

'sublime genius personified'.

Puh!

Sorry.

Genius, in my book, is finding a cure for cancer. It's not strumming a bloody guitar and singing through your nose.

So on the Blade front with me and Dad? Well, we're on opposite sides of a gaping fault-line . . . No, actually we're on different planets. This first dawned on me the day Mr Masterton in his fine red Beamer vroomed my new mate Barry over to mine to have a kick-about. Me and Barry were on the rubble of a gap-site opposite my tenement block, setting up bin bags to make goalposts, talking footie, when guess who sauntered out?

'Wotcha.' Dad blocked the ball Barry was about to boot.

He waggled a CD in Barry's face, making sure it glinted off the sun and dazzled him.

'C'mon inside 'stead of getting sweaty. Meet Bob Blade,' Dad suggested.

'Who's Bob Blade, Mr Ryan?' Barry, all snub-nosed, freckly innocence, asked the fatal question.

And oh boy, did he find out? Did he ever!

'Who's Bob Blade? You bin hidin' yourself away down a deep dark hole or something?' Dad was frogmarching Barry towards his den as he said this. 'Coz I can't believe you don't know the answer to that question, my friend. Lemme tell you once and once only, anything worth sayin' in this life? Or singin'? Or playin'? Bob Blade's nailed it in his poetry. Pithy as Shakespeare. Real as Dickens. Straight as Hemingway. Sweet as Keats. Blade's the teller of truths. The original punk. The shapeshifter. The comedian. The clown. The finger on the pulse. The song and dance man. The artist. So WHO's Bob Blade? How can you even ask me that question . . .?'

That's an edited version of the Who's Bob Blade lecture Dad laid on poor Barry. It's a soddin' miracle Barry didn't run for the hills. Because *then* Dad ensured the poor guy was thoroughly Bobwashed by exposing him to a solid afternoon of Blade's back catalogue in chronological order, sending him home with an *Essential Blade* CD. Barry's replica Brazil ball lay abandoned in the rubble over the road.

'Keep it,' he announced in school the next day. 'You can have my footie cards too if you want. Dad's gonna buy me a guitar and a "Play Like Blade" songbook.'

*

If you're still a Bob virgin yourself, a word to the wise: Stay one. I'm serious.

Don't be tempted to google Bob or browse YouTube. And don't, for goodness' sake, download bootlegs or investigate any of his 'classic' albums. Especially *Bleedin' Acid from the Soul*, or *Crash and Ride* . . .

See, Bob's one wily cat, as my dad would say. Give him an inch and he might suck you in.

After all, that's what happened to Dad when *he* was eighteen years old, and look at him now. He was a Bob virgin called Simon Anthony Ryan. Accepted to read Economics at uni, his life all mapped out like mine. Till on a weekend off from his summer sports-camp job in Oregon, he shoved stage-front at some muddy summer stoner-fest and experienced Blade live for the first time. Dad claims while Bob scanned his audience, sneering half-spoken lyrics about losers and users and club-foot fortune tellers bendin' and lendin' their ears to the wisdom of shrunken heads, their eyes locked. Blade on Simon.

And that was that.

My poor, no-longer-with-us, Granny Ryan wept

whenever she told the story of how Dad phoned her reverse charge from America. Announced he'd changed his mind about going to uni.

'Gonna live off the land for a bit, Mum. Let the sun warm me and the rain wash me clean. Jump boxcars and sing for my supper, till someone discovers me. Oh, and by the way,' Granny Ryan always used to finish up her story, 'Simon said, *"I'm Blade Ryan now. Not Simon. Don't call me that any more, mother."* Then off he went for three years. Never did make it to university.'

Not even to play support at a student gig. Never made it anywhere . . .

Actually, that's not accurate. He made it to Casualty plenty, done over by folk who didn't appreciate having mouth organs blown full throttle in their ears while they were enjoying a quiet pint.

He made it up the aisle, too. I should know. I was at the wedding, bulging under Mum's dress. Spoiling all the photos.

Mum was a brand new nurse to A&E in Leeds when Dad staggered in concussed and bleeding, in a panic about how he'd carry on making music with a broken finger and torn lip. While Student Nurse Ria Sweeney was stitching Dad's busted lip and he was squeezing her hand, she promised she'd stay with him as long as he needed her, although she'd always call him Simon.

'You look more like a Simon than a Blade to me,' she decided.

Bloody hell! I wonder if Mum had any inkling what she was letting herself in for the night she fell head over heels in A&E. Because basically she was pledging herself to a complete Loser.

Chrissake, the man's nearly fifty, and he's never had a *proper* job. You know; one you show up for five days a week.

Dad's only ever worked casual shifts:

Factory sweeper-upper,

leaflet deliverer,

site watchman . . .

And every pond-life Joe-job has only ever been temporary. Cash in hand.

That's if Dad actually reaches payday without quitting or being booted out for locking himself in the Gents with his guitar to 'figure this epic chorus brewing in my head, *maaaan*'.

Only a few weeks ago Dad even managed to get

himself ejected from Santa's grotto in John Lewis by an outrage of parents.

'Threw me into the street in my costume, man,' he complained when he slunk home. 'Was only entertaining their kiddies with my carol:

'Is Santa really Satan in disguise?
What a shame.
They sound the same.
Could Santa's jacket hide a tail?
That big red hood a set of horns
Maybe he's pure evil.
Maybe he's the devil.
And you're so small.
D' really want him down your chimney after all . . .?'

Can you believe any adult warbling *that* to smallies and seeing nothing wrong with it?

'No wonder he got the heave-ho. Glad tidings, eh?' I complained to Barry. 'There goes Mum's Christmas time off now.'

'Aw. Give over, Ro. That man is total quality, composing something like that,' Barry spluttered.

He was over to deliver his annual Bob Blade themed Christmas card. However, his handmade seasonal greeting wasn't intended for me, Barry's official best friend. Not that I'd thank him for it anyway.

'What d'you think, Ro?' Barry asked as he manoeuvred a billboard-sized dayglow painting of Bob Blade's craggy face through our front door. 'I've written the words of "Toll the Year out Weeping" inside. Y'know. Track from *Dark Days Comin' Down*?'

From behind his world-weary, pop-arted, un-Christmassy image of Bob Blade, Barry started dirging in a voice that was meant to sound like the gloomy troubadour himself. It was horrible.

'Why are you always so kind to that old git? He doesn't deserve this. Certainly not today,' I grumped, over Barry's drone and loud and clear enough for Dad to hear in his den. But I was already talking to myself.

'Woaw! You. Are. Sick. Freaking those kids,' I heard Barry congratulating Dad to the smack of hands high-fiving.

Although Barry IS my best mate – no doubt about it – I don't get him sometimes. Why does he rate such a loser? And why can't he see what a waster I'm stuck with, especially compared to his own dad? I mean, Mr M's a multi-millionaire with his own property empire. How come Barry prefers my dad's company?

I don't get my other best mate, Smillie, either. He's just as bad when it comes to rating my old man as 'one of the good guys'. Yet his dad's a top cosmetic dentist with an advert on daytime telly. Apparently this bulimic actress with influential hair off an American sitcom does the voiceover:

Do *your* teeth make you frown?
Well, just say Smillie and SMILE!

Smillie claims his dad paid half a million to hire this skinny-Minnie. And he's had his *fingers* in her mouth. How impressive is that? Yet Smillie says his dad's a 'frigging muppet. Only cares about veneers and Botox. I can't talk to him. He's just not sound like yours.'

He's just not sound like yours! Puh. Honestly, Smillie and I go back *years*. Just like Barry. The three of us have caught colds and spew-bugs off each other. We've obsessed over Pokémon. Lusted over Lara Croft. We can recite entire episodes of *Father Ted* verbatim. That's how close we are. Yet I *cannot* fathom what Smillie and Barry find so meaningful in the stoner claptrap my dad spouts. But the pair of them can't seem to keep away from the old goat.

What do my mates see in my dad that I don't?

5
PARENTS' NIGHT: THE AFTERMATH

I jump off the bus ahead of Dad, finally escaping the creepy chanting he kept up throughout our entire journey home. Rounding the corner into my street I find Barry slumped on the wall outside my flats. He's fidgeting with his phone as usual. Screen checking. Still slumped when he sees me: – 'Hey, Ro,' – half-heartedly half lifting a finger in greeting. But straightening up a moment later. All smiles.

'Oi, wotcha, Bladester. Have fun at Parents' Night? Tough going?'

Even though Dad barely blinks a greeting in response to the daft pet name he lets my mates call him, Barry slips into step beside him.

'Shit, my Old Boy was so raging with my French report he needed his angina spray. Wants me to quit school. Work for him. Thought I'd nip round. See what you'd do if you were me . . .'

I might as well be Captain Invisible here. See what I mean about Barry and Smillie? They're always 'nipping' round. Never out Dad's smoky den. You'd never guess the pair of them lived in massive cribs with ensuite ensuites and gyms and guest bedrooms and grounds.

Grounds!

Barry's mansion even comes with its own tennis court. Us Ryans don't have a *back* court to call our own. We live in a tidgy rented shoebox of a flat with a common stairway honking of chip fat and takeaways and drains. So why Barry and Smillie are happy to hang here, where they have to kip on the ratty carpet, beats me.

'We dig it here,' they tell me.

'*Dig*.' Give me a break.

'It's chilled.'

'Your dad's never on your back.'

'Too right. And you can talk to Bladester.'

'Like *talk* talk.'

'You're lucky.'

Lucky, is it?

*

Believe me, I explain how Ryan family life is far from brilliant:

How we're broke. How Mum's run into the ground working all the hours God sends.

But Barry and Smillie can't see past old leather kecks.

They hang on Dad's every word:

Should I grow my hair long this summer, Bladester?

I've been wearing the same boxers for two days. Should I change them, Bladester?

The pair of them even show genuine interest in Dad's pointless song-writing.

'So. Written anything new, Bladester?' Barry's asking while he trails Dad into his den tonight.

An hour later the pair of them are still holed up in there. By this time music drifts out. Bursts of laughter. Snatches of low conversation.

Me? I'm left pacing the hall, wishing Barry would come out so we could conduct a debrief about how tight Miss Sweet's jumper was tonight. Stuff like that. My nose is bothering me too, of course. Well, it's out of joint.

'Barry's *my* mate, actually,' I seethe outside Dad's den. Seethe out loud, by the way, which is weird in itself. Then, as if hissing, 'Why not find someone your own age,' into this air wasn't weird enough, I blurt this on top:

'That's the story of my life.'

Only when these word are out, half sung, do I realise they've been looping inside my head ever since I plonked beside Dad on the bus.

It's the sto-ree of ma life.

I'm riled. *Nothing* is more annoying than having a tune you can't identify stuck in your nut. Drives you mad. Drives *me* mad anyway.

That's the stor-ee of ma life

Oh, yeah. That's the stor-ee of ma life.

'What's that song? It could be a genuine Bob Blade song, but it's a sweeter singer singing. Chrissake. Look at me: I'm whispering to a door,' I whisper. 'Dad does stuff like that . . .' I keep whispering, even as I'm opening the music library Smillie put on our computer. Sound like a creepy mentalist, so I do. But I can't stop singing under my breath while I sift the titles in the computer songlist: *'Stor-ee of ma life . . .'*

With no luck on iTunes or Spotify, I google the title

next, chanting the lyric like a spell to bring its creator up on screen.

'Catchy, innit, Ro? Hey. What you looking up? Thought you knew everything?'

I'm so engrossed in my detective work, Barry's knuckling the top of my head before I realise he's breathing down my neck. So he won't twig there's a fact he knows I don't, I bring up the St Andrew's Uni Prospective Students' homepage from my Favourites.

'Just double-checking the grade I'll need to do Physics. Came up at Parents' Night,' I lie, flicking off the monitor before Barry frowns any more suspiciously. 'How 'bout you?' I change the subject.

'How 'bout me what?' Barry shrugs.

'Tonight. Did Stat tell your folks about the Wolfwoman cartoon in her pigeonhole –?

Barry's frown deepens while I'm speaking. He shakes his head. Holds out the flat of his hand.

'Listen.' He cocks his head towards the door.

'Zat why your dad kicked off?'

'*Shhh. Listen.*'

Barry's edging away from me. His head's still tilted, face still crumpled in a frown. But it's a smiley, faraway frown.

'Bladester's added rhythm guitar . . .'

Using the same hand he held up to silence me, Barry plucks invisible strings. Under his breath he murmurs to the tune I can just about hear over the strumming.

'. . . *Hung my head and I walked away.*

That's the story of my life . . .'

'Good, innit?' Barry slaps my shoulder like he's congratulating me.

'See ya, Bladester,' he calls but there's no answer from the den.

Just strumming and humming and mouth-organy wheezing.

'Says he'll finish the whole song by tomorrow.' Barry bobs his head towards the sound. Then he makes to cuff me on the chin.

'I'm offski. *Another dismal day on the cruel highway.*' Out on the landing, Barry's voice lofts to the skylight three floors above. Singing as he takes the stairs, the patter of his descending feet keep time with my dad's guitar: '*That's the stor-ee of my life . . .*'

'So you're not leaving school after all?' I call down the stairwell.

'Nah. Bladester says just keep on truckin',' Barry's

voice echoes all around me. 'Says if I follow dreams, not bread, life'll sort itself.'

Puh! Follow dreams, not bread.

'Mince! You can't eat bloody dreams.'

OK. I'm talking to myself again, but it's half ten and I've had no dinner. I'm sour. Tired. Starving. Three good reasons to justify the way I snap when I hear Mum's key in the door.

'There's no food in this stupid house, Mum –'

I'm well out of order, the way I block Mum. Gangle over her. Can't stand myself for what I do, but I can't help myself either.

Why is that?

Why is it you act the complete opposite of how you want to when you're really happy or relieved to see someone sometimes? I've always been that way with Selina Sutherland, who of course I realise is utterly out of my league, but who I've had the hots for since I was about six. She sashays along a corridor towards me in her sprayed-on blouse. And what do I do? Kid on there are fascinating things happening over her shoulder. I never say hi, even though I want to prostrate myself at her feet:

I LOVE YOU, YOU'RE SO CLEVER. OUR CHILDREN WILL BE PRODIGIES . . . And right now standing over Mum I really want to give her a hug. *The teachers gave me good reports, Mum. Wish you'd been there.*

Instead I thrust a crumbed-up jar of Marmite under Mum's nose.

'I'm starving and *he* was a complete dickhead tonight.'

Even as I'm flourishing my arm in the direction of Dad's den, my voice rising, I clock how pale Mum looks round the eyes. Even paler than normal. How dead-beat she is, slowly unbuttoning her raincoat and easing her feet from her shoes.

I should be taking the shopping Mum's humphed two flights of stairs. Should be unpacking it. *Sit down. I'll sort this.* Instead I let Mum heft her bags on to the kitchen table.

'You promised you'd come tonight. Where were you?'

I follow Mum from the breadbin to the fridge, nagging her with questions, even though I know, and she knows I know, why she let me down.

'When Simon got sacked from that warehouse . . . Well, you know the money situation, pet –' Mum pauses and for a moment the only sound in the flat is Dad's soft music. Then she shrugs. 'I'm doing Casualty shifts back to back with my regular ones. No choice.'

Mum's sticking something ready-made in the microwave. Between the guff from its fan and Dad's electric guitar wailing, I can hardly hear her.

'Anyway –' Mum puts a plate and a knife and fork on the kitchen table. Pours me a glass of milk. 'Your report was all good.'

As she makes this statement, Mum lays hers hand on my cheek, waiting till I raise my eyes to meet hers before she takes it away.

'I'm sorry, Rory. Let's catch up in the morning, eh? Properly. But I need to have a word with his nibs . . .'

Mum closes the door kitchen door behind her. Carefully.

But I know she's in Dad's den when his strumming turns to screaming feedback. That's the sound of his guitar strings complaining about being propped too carelessly against an amp.

Ding ding pings the microwave.

Like a mustering call for silence.

Two heartbeats of silence.

Before the voices rumble.

Engage.

Ding ding. Round One.

I take my meal to the table. Shloop it from the plastic tray to my plate.

'Simon, why exactly did they sack you? Couldn't you just have tholed the job for the money? For Rory?'

Mum's voice is cracked. Too weary to be angry.

I'm not hungry any more.

6

NEW MORNING

Next morning Mum's already in the shower when I stagger to the bathroom door.

'The fallin' leaves,' she's belting out, *'. . . are gentle as string –'*

'It's *spring* not string. Gonna be long?' I rap the door. 'You're murdering a Bob Blade song by the way.'

'Rubbish. George Harrison, no?'

'Ask Dad.'

'He's out job-hunting. And you just want me out of the bathroom, sunshine.'

Before Mum emerges in a billow of steam I've nicked Bob Blade's *Just Born Daybreak* CD from the wonky, chronologically arranged shelf in Dad's den. Cued track one.

'I'm never wrong.' I pat Mum's towelled head as I disappear into the bathroom myself, leaving her with country-period Bob Blade yodelling through the flat.

A weird thing I've noticed about Mum is how she tends to be in a sunshiny mood the morning after she's had a set-to with Dad. Must be something in the nature of my parents' particular chemistry, but they seem to crave regular barneys to re-cement whatever it is that holds them together. Maybe all married couples behave like this.

I don't know.

It's not like I'd be comfortable discussing a topic like that with Barry or Smillie: marriage. My folks disappearing into their bedroom and making up overnight . . . I don't know if it's a general guy thing, but we just don't venture along avenues like that in our particular friendship, although I suppose deep down we know we could. And would. If we had to . . .

Smillie, mind you, can only talk about feelings that are crotch related, which is strange considering how let-it-all-hang-out-under-your-organic-cheesecloth-smock his mum is. Barry, on the other hand, actually sort of *half* revealed emotional turmoil a few months back. It was a blink and you miss it chink in his lad-armour, though. Two of us were down in his basement playing air hockey. One minute I was beating him and the next I was being ear-clipped by the puck. Barry had super-charged slammed it so hard he gouged a fist of plaster out the wall behind me.

'That's for shaggin' your bimbo secretary,' Barry spluttered.

'Christ sake! My ear –' My automatic protest petered out while my mouth was still challenging Barry: 'What bimbo secretary . . .?'

Then the penny dropped.

'Shit, Baz. Your old *man* . . .?' By which time Barry had already retrieved the puck.

'Forget it,' he clipped. His focus was back on the game.

So, although Barry and Smillie must know I live with parents whose marriage is a bucking bronco, only black-haired Annette Muir has been privy to an actual admission from the horse's mouth. Don't ask me why, but it was the second thing I whispered to her that morning when she slumped down next to me after the chaplain had embarrassed her into admitting her parents had split.

And I only revealed, 'I can't believe *my* folks are still together. They keep tearing into each other, then making up. It's insane in my house,' so she'd have to lean in to hear me and wouldn't clock the head to foot critical scrutiny she was being subjected to from every Sixth Former in Pastoral Care.

'But that's sweet,' was Annette's response that morning. 'At least it means your folks are still in love and always will be. My mum and dad stopped talking when I was ten,' she told me. And then said she came home from school one day and her mum was gone for good.

How tough is that?

Anyway, returning to *this* morning, *despite* the empty whisky bottle and two glasses pushed to the side of the kitchen table, Mum's bright-eyed and bushy-tailed enough to waft a plate of French toast in front of me when I join her in the kitchen.

'Ambassador, you spoil me,' I kid Mum. 'Hot chocolate too?'

'Well, you'll be on your own tonight.'

'Dad'll be here.'

'Better not be. He's promised things'll change –' Mum pulls yesterday's paper out from under the whisky. It's open on the recruitment pages.

I read the ad circled in red.

'Cleanliness operative? That's a puke-swabber at *your* hospital. No way, Mum. Dad's nails are a walking MRSA epidemic . . .'

'They're desperately short-staffed. And *we're* desperate for money. I told Simon to take anything going.'

Out in the hall Mum's groaning like an arthritic pensioner. Means she's working her feet into her nurse shoes.

'Your dad's waiting at Human Resources for the manager to come in. He should get a start today.'

'What about references?'

'They're desperate right now, Rory.' Mum pecks the top of my head. 'Unlike you, Star of St Bernard's.'

Although it's just us two, Mum whispers, 'He'd never say, but I know Simon would be proud last night.'

I think not.

Though I don't flex my debating skills on Mum. Well, she's left for work anyway. And she was only doing her nursy. Putting a temporary dressing on the sore that's me and Dad. Same as she patched up her own problems last night.

'*Just Born Daybreak,* indeed,' I grump at the CD I've remembered to shove back among Dad's precious Bob Blade collection. I've my schoolbag shoulder-slung and I'm opening the front door when a hand lands on my shoulder.

'Oi! Place for everything, Einstein.'

For a split second I think the guy who's grabbed me is myself sporting joke facial hair, but when I'm marched back to Dad's den and ordered to put back *Just Born Daybreak*, 'In between my *Native Heart Songs* and *Blade's Rapier* please, Einstein, if you don't mind,' I know this bossyboots is just daddy dearest wearing my spare school trousers and no make-up.

'You're not here,' I gulp.

'No, *you're* not here. Chop, chop. Dada needs the house to himself,' he says, steering me on to the landing.

'Thought Mum sent you off to find work.' I resist Dad's efforts to shut the front door on me.

'She did. I went. Suits told me to cut my nails. To clean shit!'

Click. The door's closed on me.

'I'm a music man.' Through the frosted glass, Dad's voice is sour. 'Just trying to figure out some songs,' he mutters, more to himself than to me. 'And I'm on the right train at last. In my mind, man. Ain't getting off to mop no floor for no one. Not till I reach my destination . . .'

Dad's distorted shadow shrinks from view as his words fade.

What bollocks. Train journeys of the mind.

'Puh!'

By the time I'm out on the landing stairs Dad's started belting out lusty scales to himself:

'La la la la la la laaaaaaaa–h!'

I can still hear him when I reach the bottom landing. Till Mr Moran (the Moron, Dad calls him. Not to his face) who rents the flat below, and works as a bouncer in the casino, bangs something hard and metallic against a pipe. It knells through the stairwell like a final warning.

Stepping into the rain, part of me's thinking serve Dad right if Moran shows him the business end of his knuckleduster. However, I pause at the entrance to our tenement, straining my ears. Just to make sure Dad's put a lid on the vocal gymnastics.

Much quieter.

Though not silent.

I catch the strum of Dad's guitar, the thin harmony of his mouth organ. He's playing that tune again. The catchy one from last night.

. . . *It's the story of my life* . . .

So I take it to the bus stop with me. Carry it into school. The soundtrack to a very odd day.

7

TUMMY TROUBLE

It's Selina Sutherland's fault I skip the occasional line of working during Maths.

You see, before the lesson starts, she slinks into the seat in front of me. It's the one Annette normally likes to take so I can feed her whispered answers while Stat's bawling in her face.

'Was that your dad last night?' Selina whips round and blings me a smile. 'Cuz my mum says he's like Steve Tyler'n'Alice Cooper rolled into one. I just thought he looked *wild*. Pretty different from you,' she coos. I think. Her unexpected nearness has turned the space between us into hot buzzing static filled with birds tweeting and rainbows twinkling like xylophones. What I *can* confirm though, is when Selina turns back round and smoothes her skirt over her bum, it fits the shape of her curves like a second skin. *Hubba hubba,* I can hear Barry's voice panting in my head. No wonder. When Selina leans forward her bra is completely outlined through her blouse. Could reach out and undo it in a heartbeat . . .

As soon as the lesson begins, Selina props her cheek on her hand and goes into this sexy little routine every time she goes to copy something down. Out pouts her bottom lip.

Whhoooophhhh!

She blows away this irksome strand of honey-blondeness. No wonder I'm struggling with my *x* and *y*' s. Poetry in motion, Selina's ritual is. So mesmerising I'd contentedly goggle it till the Big Chief decides it's taxi for Rory.

'Quotient, Selina? And stop fussing with your hair, dear. You've sent Rory Ryan into a trance. His little eyes are spinning behind his little Harry Potter specs.'

Now here's the curious thing – and by the way, my specs are not Harry Potter-shaped – Stat's taught me Maths for two years, right? Yet this put-down is the very, *very* first comment I've ever heard her make that wasn't . . . well, *mathematical*. She's *so* impersonal, Smillie's convinced she's a robo-teacher.

'How else,' he's forever insisting, 'd'you explain that beard and mismatching eyes?'

Not to mention her chilling, metallic drone, I'm thinking to myself as Stat intones, 'I'm surprised you've the gall to sit here in my class after the way your father spoke to me last night,' her whiskery face looming over my own. 'I was extremely upset, and you can tell him that. Inappropriate conduct clearly runs in your family,' she concludes as she beckons me to follow her to the Smartboard.

'Let's see how far your mind's wandered to figures that have nothing to do with A-LEVEL MATH-E-MATICS!!!' Stat's Dalek-in-a-rage rising pitch has me stabbing so nervously at her keyboard, I delete the entire screenful of numbers everyone's been copying down.

'Thanks. Double homework.' Selina isn't cooing at me any more. 'Keep your eyes to yourself next time, Sadboy,' she scowls, flouncing out the classroom ahead of me.

In the corridor Annette's hand lies briefly against my back.

'Aw, Rory, that was horrible. And what's your dad's behaviour got to do with you, anyway? Was he at Parents' Night? Never saw him. Shame. I've a Music lesson now,' she calls over her shoulder before she's swept away in the opposite direction from me by the period change scrum. Since I definitely *don't* have a Music lesson, and am keen to debunk Smillie's robo-teacher theory, I seek out my mates.

'. . . See. Stat slagged me off. That proves she's human. And for your information robots can't be "upset", Smillie.'

'*Millenium Man*?'

'Just a dire film. And they don't seek revenge.'

'*Westworld*? Yul Brynner? Cowboy robot? He seeks revenge *big* time.'

'Hey, and what about *Doctor Who*? It's full of robots with emotions,' Barry chips in. 'It's pretty real.'

Oh give me strength!: *Doctor Who is fiction, you Rice Krispy-brains,* I'm itching to let rip at my mates, but I keep my cool. Draw on my debating skills instead.

'Point of information. Stat's proved to me she has feelings.'

'For you, Ro?' Barry wolf-whistles. Tastefully pumps his pelvis at me.

'Dad told her to keep her beard on last night,' I press on. 'Howled like a wolf at her. She was upset –'

Well, that's the end of that conversation. You

can't proceed with a debate when the opposition's hyperventilating.

'Oh, that Bladester –' Barry's face-down, beating his fists off the school yard.

'The man's so –' By the time Smillie sinks to his knees, he's sobbing with mirth.

'Howled like a wolf. Epic. Oh, hang on.' Barry, still prostrate, gropes about for his ringing mobile.

'Hey, and speak of the devil. Rory's just telling up how you're in Wolfwoman's bad books. Whassup? Finished your song?'

'Is that my *dad*?' I talk across Barry. Rude of me I know, but I'm dumbstruck here, and not just because my hopeless old man's managed to call a *mobile phone*.

What's really pulled the rug from under my feet is realising he's apparently involved in something with my mates.

Something that has Barry listening intently. Suddenly sober.

Something that excludes me. Not that that's necessarily an issue. Barry and Smillie and I are mates, not clones. Okay. So we converge on things like air-hockey and the appreciation of Angelina Jolie and *Father Ted*, but we diverge on plenty more. On the point of Bond movies, for instance. And Bond girls. On the merit of rock star computer games. On the significance of rock stars and seeing them live in concert. Come to think of it, I probably diverge more from Barry and Smillie than they do from each other. Especially when it comes to music. They claim – same as Dad – that they can't live without it. *How can anyone?* they say. Yet it's something I just can't get into at all. I *never* listen to music off my own bat for enjoyment. Never have.

'Makes you really, really weird that, you know. Like sad weird. Not cool weird,' Smillie likes to inform me every so often. 'You never even whistle or hum like everyone else in the world. And I've *never* heard you sing –'

'Oh man, I have. So've you. You must have blanked it out your memory. Wish I could!' The last time Smillie raised this subject, Barry was quick to jump in. 'D'you not remember standing next to Ro in assembly that time Stanton went walkabout to check everyone was belting out the school song?' Barry was shuddering. 'Christ, Ro did something with his throat that'd scare hungry seagulls off a pizza crust. I think there's a birth defect kicking in that makes Ro different from the rest of us.'

*

As I say, normally I'm ho-hum about my mates being on ploys that leave me out, but today, when Barry cocks his head at Smillie, 'C'mere,' then nods him close to listen in, I bristle. As soon as Smillie scuttles over to butt his ear to Barry's phone, he starts waggling his arse in the air.

'Oi, what's going on with you guys?'

I hunker down myself. Try to edge between Barry and Smillie. Hear what they're hearing. But they lock against me.

'Listen. Think we'll just come over.' Barry cuts the call. 'Y'up for that, Smiler?'

'She say "try". I say "I do". Well ah give up with boys like you –' Smillie sings in reply, circling his index finger at Barry's face. 'It's too good, Bazzer.'

'Giving me tummy trouble, it's so good.' Barry parts his legs wide. Trumpets a rancid, two-tone fart. 'Better take the rest of the day off, case I parp one out in French.'

'Oi! You're not going home?' I jog after Barry and Smillie, firing questions, but the pair of them don't stop moving to answer till they're beyond the school gates.

'Chill, Ro. You'll blow a fuse in your big brain.' Barry

pats my head. 'We're on Music business. Not your thang. So just say me'n'Smiles here had to run home with *dy-a-ree-a* if anyone asks. Geddit? Run? Runs?'

'But don't say we've run to *your* home.' Smillie boxes my solar plexus with a quick one-two that brings me to my knees. It's his own sweet way of reassuring me we're all still mates.

Even though he and Barry are offski.

To do something with *my* dad.

8

A GOOD DAY'S WORK

But don't feel sorry for me or anything like that.

Smillie's just free with his fists. Nothing personal. Goes with being christened Oliver and having to wear a mummy-knitted uniform to school. After a few deep breaths on my hands and knees, I'm right as rain.

In fact, with the guys out my hair, you wouldn't *believe* the work I get through.

I finish all my Maths homework, scoot through a Physics past paper, then romp a dozen '**Scientist! Challenge Yourself Further**' Chemistry tests.

No one jogs my arm while I'm writing, or analyses whether Miss Sweet's tits look pert, melony or lonely today. So no wonder I'm in a top mood by the time I get home. Early, thanks to not needing to dawdle at the bus stop. Specifically so Barry and Smillie can pretend to ignore the girls they deliberately miss buses to see.

I don't pause to hang up my blazer. Just burst into the

sitting room, announcing as I throw myself on the sofa, 'Honey, I'm home –' in the kind of dipstick voice you only EVER use when you assume you have a house to yourself.

I don't, of course.

Barry and Smillie are at the computer, flanking Dad. The guys are radiating out huge salty waves of embarrassment for me.

'Hey, Ro.' By refusing to meet my eyes, I presume Barry's trying to save face on my behalf.

'Awright?' Smillie frowns at the carpet like there's a dog-shit steaming there.

'Oi, some of us are working,' Dad snaps, acting his age for once.

Well, I know when I'm not wanted. So I slink off. Shower. Manage eighty sit-ups. Polish my school shoes.

From the sitting room, there's abnormally little noise. Just an occasional rumble of voices. Snatches of music. That 'Story of My Life' song again. Drifting through the flat at low volume.

Outside dusk falls. No one quits the sitting room to come and find me. No one even answers when I stick my head round the door.

'Cuppa anyone? Marmite sandwich?'

When I notice it's turned dark outside and my stomach's rumbling up a storm, I announce, 'I'll buy everyone fish'n'chips.'

No one thanks me.

It pours all the way to the chippy. Teems it on the way back. I run fast as I can, juggling four fish suppers so they don't scorch the skin off my palms. Turning into my street I bump into Barry and Smillie.

'Why you doing out in the rain, Dumb-Nuts?' Smillie automatically yanks the hood of my anorak over my face, drawing the toggle as tight as it goes. 'Shame you can't be arsed with music. We'd a hot recording session there.' Smillie bonks my head affectionately. 'Me'n'Baz were producing.'

With my hands full I can't shift the hood. Have to splammo-jerk my head back a few times before Barry untoggles me.

'Yeah, Ro. Quality session.'

Barry flashes a CD in front of my eyes. When its surface catches the reflection of the streetlight above us I'm blinded. I sense, rather than see, Barry shaking his head at the soggy parcels I offer him and Smillie.

'Aw sorry, mate. Appreciate like, but no food in Dad's motor. Dems de rules.' Barry cocks his head at an approaching four by four.

'Gotta go anyway.' Barry slaps my shoulder so hard I nearly drop the fish suppers.

'Double chips for you and Bladester. Get him to play his song. Even *you* gotta like it.' Barry's calling from the car, still flashing the CD. 'It's mint.'

I can just about hear Barry over the drumming rain on my anorak hood. Then Mr M's wheels backspin the contents of the kerbside gutter into my face.

9

BLADE AWOL

By the time I poke about to salvage a morsel of haddock that doesn't slime in puddle gravy, I can't face eating. What is it about chippy fish and chips? Unless you wire in right away, they turn your stomach. Ugh! I plop what I'd planned to scoff myself on top of the sog I'm arranging for Dad. Blast it in the micro.

'Hot! Hot! Hot!' I announce, head turned to avoid inhaling any steam off the reheated fish supper. I'm sparing you a description of the smell.

And wouldn't you know, Dad's spared too.

His leather coat's gone. And his cig tin. I check his den. Bedroom. Notice his favourite acoustic guitar's missing too.

Don't know why I waste time looking about for a note. Disappearing without warning is something Dad does.

Hours. Days. Nights. Weeks.

'I'm the rollin' stone that gathers no moss, me. Man

o' the road,' is how he excuses himself. Afterwards. To me. To Mum.

And she always puts him right: 'That's not true, Simon. You're just a silly, selfish man at times. One who won't grow up.'

Mum and I didn't see Dad for seven months once. Drowning his sorrows in a dockside pub after yet another sacking, and probably too scared to come home and tell Mum, he got chatting with this nautical bloke. His new barstool buddy turned out to be, not only a fellow Bob Blade obsessive, but a short-staffed Entertainments Officer desperate to recruit a supper cabaret act. Dad set sail on the Twilight Tours cruiser without leaving a forwarding address. A year on the ocean waves he'd have been gone if the grey panthers he was entertaining every night hadn't mutinied over the dearth of Keane and Coldplay songs in his repertoire.

A long-term disappearing act like that kind of puts Dad's five-minute absence into perspective, doesn't it? I'm more bothered he's left an amp humming in the middle of the room, plugged to his bass. Its tone clashes spine-shiveringly with the fuzz-buzz off Dad's eight-track. Still hooked up to the computer, it blinks and flashes like a miniature Las Vegas.

'Just leave your life on standby.' I'm tempted to pull the PC plug at the mains. But the cyber-perfectionist in me itches for systematic closedown:

WORD.

Save.

Close.

PRO-TOOLS.

Save.

Close.

So far, so good: one by one the open programs clogging the bottom of the screen plip clear. What I'm actually *saving*, I don't check. I'm only interested to see everything tidying itself away. Neatly. Into the desktop.

'No problemo,' I congratulate myself. A bit too soon, given I'm dealing with our glitchy old PC. Down to the last open program, and the bloody thing's refusing to close.

DO YOU WISH TO REVERT TO LATEST VERSION?

It might as well be shrieking at me.

Latest version of what? Shit!

I restore Dad's file to full screen size. Then actually reel back when I see what plings up: a song.

A song set out like sheet music an orchestra would play.

I mean, there's a treble and a bass clef, a time signature and guitar tab. Then all the hoppy little notes you see on compositions by real composers like Mozart and Beethoven and Gary Barlow and Sir Elton John, with crotchets and quavers and tadpoles and mini-mes or whatever they're called dancing and swinging or balancing on telephone-line-like wires strung across the screen. I don't read music, but even *I* can tell whatever's on this file looks . . . well . . .

Story of My Life.

Words and Music by Blade Ryan.

This certainly doesn't look like Dad's usual scribble on a torn-off cigarette-box lid. Scrawled in some pub. Illegible the next morning. That's how most of his compositions begin. And end.

Unfinished Symphonies, Mum calls them. But what Dad's put on the computer looks:

'Professional.' My talking-to-myself-like-Dad-does voice is full of surprise. 'So *that's* why Barry and Smillie were helping . . .'

All sorts of feelings are jostling in the region of my neck where my throat meets my collarbone. The feelings form a lump. It whispers:

*'**I'm** good at tech stuff too. Better than Barry and Smillie . . . I wish . . . I could've. All Dad had to do was ask . . .'*

When I've printed off every page of Dad's song, I lay it out on the floor.

'Is it any good?' I wonder, wishing I *could* read music. Wishing I knew one string on Dad's bass from the other so I could pluck out the melody line he's composed to see if this printed tune is still the same as the one that's been worming into my head since Parents' Night. If only I understood music I'd be able to hear how it fits the lyrics I read aloud in the empty flat:

VERSE:

GOTTA LET YOU GO

GOTTA SHRINK THE LINE

SEZ A KID WHO COULD BE MY SON

I SEZ 'WHAT?'

HE SEZ 'SO!

CLEAR YOUR LOCKER, YOU'RE FREE TO GO.

WE'LL SEND YOUR PAYCHEQUE ON NEXT WEEK.

GOOD LUCK.'

MY HEAD HANGS LOW AND I WALK AWAY.

CHORUS:

THERE'S THE STORY OF MY LIFE.

THAT'S THE STORY OF MY LIFE.

VERSE:

KINDA STARTED OFF

WHEN I SAT IN SCHOOL

ALL MY TEACHERS YELLED ME DOWN

MIZ GRAY SEZ 'TRY.'

I SEZ 'I DO.'

'WELL, I'VE NO PATIENCE FOR KIDS LIKE YOU,' SEZ SHE,

'BOY, YOU'RE TOO DARN SLOW. KEEP OUT MY SIGHT

'FORE I KNOCK SOME BRAINS IN YOUR HOLLOW SKULL.'

CHORUS:

IT'S THE STORY OF MY LIFE.

THAT'S THE STORY OF MY LIFE.

VERSE:

SO I QUIT MY BOOKS

WROTE A BUNCH OF SONGS

WENT TO PLAY THEM TO THE MAN

'ANY GOOD?' SEZ I.

'NEXT!' SEZ HE.

'CAN'T SAY THESE TUNES APPEAL TO ME

AND YOUR FACE AIN'T CUTE ENOUGH. YOU JUST WON'T SELL

SEND THE NEXT BOY IN WHEN YOU CLOSE MY DOOR.'

CHORUS:

WAS THE STORY OF MY LIFE.

THERE'S THE STORY OF MY LIFE.

VERSE:

THEN I HIT THE ROAD

ME AND MY GUITAR

BAR TO BAR AND TOWN TO TOWN

'SING BLUES?' I SEZ,

'PAY IN FOOD NOT BREAD.

ROCK, FOLK AND COUNTRY TOO.'

BUT THEM LANDLORDS SHRUG: 'WE GOT POLES AND GIRLS,

KARAOKE, POOL AND DARTS.

YOU'RE OUTA TIME AND YOU'RE OUTA TOUCH.'

CHORUS:

THAT'S THE STORY OF MY LIFE.

IT'S THE STORY OF MY LIFE.

VERSE:

SO I'M DOWN AND OUT

AND MY SPIRIT'S BEAT

I TRUDGE HOMEBOUND, HEAD HUNG LOW

I SEZ 'MA?'

PA SEZ 'NO!

SLING YOUR HOOK. GET OUT. GIT. GO.

CAN'T HAVE YOU WITH YOUR SLINKIN', DRINKIN' WAYS.

PUT YOUR LIFE ON TRACK, THEN WE'LL TAKE YOU BACK.'

THAT THE STORY OF MY LIFE.

IT'S THE STORY OF MY LIFE.

VERSE:

NOW I'M ON MY KNEES

AND I PRAY FOR HELP

I DON'T KNOW WHICH WAY TO TURN.

'LORD' SEZ I.

'LORD?' SEZ I.

STILL DON'T KNOW IF HE'S CAUGHT MY CRY

IF HE HEARD ME PRAY: 'SO WHAT DO I DO NOW?'

'NOTHER DISMAL DAY ON LIFE'S CRUEL HIGHWAY.

CHORUS.

YOU HEARD THE STORY OF MY LIFE.

THAT'S THE STORY OF MY LIFE.

REPEAT CHORUS AND FADE.

'Boo hoo. Someone's feeling sorry for himself.' I'm crouched over Dad's song, a knee-jerk sneer my typical default.

What kind of son does that make me? There's a voice in my head needling an accusation as I scoop Dad's pages up. Block them together.

'Hey, I printed off that stuff you were writing,' I imagine telling Dad whenever he blows back home. There again, I might not bother. It's not like Dad'd notice I'd done anything for him.

'*And that's the story of ma life. It's the story of ma life,*' I find myself singing.

Now, what's *scientifically* interesting about me doing that, is that Dad's clearly composed something catchy enough to make me feel I've known it forever. Something anthemic, I suppose, like one of those tunes that hurtle on an unstoppable collision course to a sing-along chorus you anticipate from the very first note. I might not understand music, but I've been drip-fed enough of it to recognise something similarly hurtling in at least two of the lines my dad's written.

And for the *only* time in my life, here I am: *desperate* to check out something my loser of a dad has done.

10

FIFTEEN MINUTE BOB

I'm still up when Dad comes home, and I've managed to recover a vocal of his song. Must have listened to it a dozen times over. Dad's voice. Sweet and rough. On lead and harmony, over two or three layers of guitar, then a burst of chaotic, laddish *ooh-ahhing* before everything fades to whoops and handclaps.

Crikey-mikey, if Barry and Smillie think that racket they're making amounts to singing, I could have joined in with them on that bit. 'Stead of sitting in the kitchen like a splam . . . I can't help thinking.

Then a scuffling from the landing distracts me.

'Where's m'bastard keyhole?' a voice slurs before Dad careens backwards into the sitting room. Beer and sweat belch in with him. The reek of pubs.

'Someone's moved that lock.'

You'd think from the way Dad tries to balance that our living room carpet was laid on choppy water. I'm seasick just watching him veer to stay vertical, his eyes gliding in their sockets like a pair of tipsy goldfish swimming round a bowl in opposite directions to each other. His pupils are glassy, his lids drooped nearly as low as the comma of ash dangling from his mouth.

'Oi, Rory'sh here. Quick –' Dad cups his hands to his face when he spots me. Yells in the direction of the hall. About two footsteps away.

'Hoi! Sez there's Rory. C'min.'

Dad sweeps an arm up and over his head to welcome whoever I hear kicking and bashing about the hall like it's suddenly clogged with snares and cymbals and hi-hats.

Shit. Surely, SURELY not.

'In here, maaan.'

When Dad repeats his arm sweep with added vigour, the effort lurches him sideways over the settee.

'You're wellied,' I hiss over Dad's upside-down face while I'm saving Mum's favourite cushion from a fag burn. 'And you better not have brought . . .'

Before I manage to haul Dad upright and confiscate anything flammable – 'Ooopla!' – this denim-clad gnome-man springs in front of me like a jack-in-the-box. Tries to winch Dad off the settee. Ends up collapsed on top of Dad himself, so that instead of two blokes monged out their boxes, it looks like there's an octopus dressed up for a Status Quo tribute night flailing about on the floor.

Half the octopus, I'm gutted to see, is Dad's bad-news ex-drummer from way-back-when. Levon, Dad calls him. After Levon Helm. Drummer, singer, guitar and mandolin player for The Band. The Band who played loud and wild and on the same circuit as Bob Blade way back in Canada in the good ol' swingin', amphetamine-fuelled sixties blah, blah, blah . . . like *anyone* cares donkey's years on. Dad's 'Levon' isn't Levon, either. His name's Mickey Mack.

Bad News and Trouble, Mum calls him. She's barred Mickey for life. From me. Dad. From ever darkening our door again.

Yet here he is, darkening the carpet with the can of Guinness he's opened upside down.

'D'ya trip me, Levon?' Dad uses Mickey's shoulders to lever himself upright. Mickey uses Dad's head to do the same. Five minutes later they're still tangling, going nowhere.

'Firewater?' Mickey pants, fumbling a bottle from

down the front of his jeans. 'Put hairs on your manhood.'

Mickey, I realise, is waving the bottle at me, his tongue slipping in and out the space where most people his age still have teeth.

'Hey, junior,' he gurns, his hands beating time on a set of imaginary drums, 'lot o' water under the bridge since I last got a call to scud the tom-toms for daddio.'

A summer of flash floods wouldn't be enough, I'm tempted to snipe at Mickey. Pummel him while he's down. I'm a lot, lot bigger than he is now. Apart from his biceps. They bulge beneath the hacked-off sleeves of his stone-washed denim jacket, each one bigger than a baby's head. Must still be drumming.

'Dad tell you I'd my stomach pumped? After I sucked your coke-stash out of that sherbet dip? Lucky Mum's a nurse.' I cast Mickey my deepest scowl.

'Aw, we're quits now, me'n'you. I served three years bird, thanks to your mum's clipe to Crimestoppers. And listen, on the subject of The Night Nurse –' Mickey sobers up '– Ria *is* out, man? Cuz her and me'll never be quits.' With a shudder Mickey bounces off the sitting room walls into the hall. While he's bashing about outside, I tackle Dad.

'If he's staying, he's not sleeping in my room – Mum'll freak.'

'Shhhhhh.' Dad points at my crotch. 'Always something twisting your treat-me-gentles, Einstein.' He chortles drunkenly as he scuttles across the carpet. When he reaches the chair at the computer, he works his way up, hand over hand, till he's lolled over the keyboard.

'Levon's here because he is the bezz drummer I know, and tonight I –' Dad pauses. He's staring into the computer screen the way you'd gaze at a crystal ball, eventually flicking his fingers star-wide. 'After all these years – *Pow!* I've seen through the hazy lookin'-glass. Bob Blade talks about that, y'know,' he whispers. '*The hazy lookin'-glass*. Songwriting. I've peered through it m'self now. Yeah, Levon?'

'Dunno. Still to hear this frigging song you keep nipping my ear about,' Mickey splutters though the milk he's swigging straight from the carton. 'Howzbout we get my sticks going 'fore that horny barmaid down the Swallow loses the notion for a heap of Mickey-love . . .'

Ugh.

I'm only grateful that Dad begins harmonising loosely over his computer vocal before Mickey goes into much more detail about barmaids and swallowing. By the second chorus, Mickey's groped down his jeans for a pair of drumsticks. Head cocked like he's working on one of the safecrack jobs he used to boast about, he builds a rhythm on the edge of our dining room table.

The milk's bad enough but if Mum saw this! I nearly interrupt Mickey. I shove one of his drums in front of him to bash the daylights out of rather than the furniture. But his eyes are squinched shut.

Doka dok DUNN Doka dok DUNN

'Howzat, man? Beefy enough?' Mickey shouts over a blur of sticks. They're belting Mum's table so hard now, splinters fly.

'*Big* song, man.' Mickey keeps the rhythm beating after the song fades. Till suddenly he stops. He punches the air with a clenched first.

'Toucha Bob Blade's "Back-lot Gutter Blues" in the verses. "Travellin 'n' Truckin'" in the chorus. And you know what? I see you 'n' me. *"How ya doing, New York?"* Some main stage. Crowds yelling your fuck-off chorus back in our faces . . .'

Mickey reaches across the table with his sticks.

'Feel those hairs on your neck tingling, man?'

He batters a mini drum roll on Dad's nearest arm.

Ouch! I'm wincing, though Dad doesn't flinch. Doesn't look especially pleased with Mickey's reaction, either. He rasps his hands up over his stubbled chin. Knackered and washed-out he looks. Putty-faced. Far, far older than he really is.

'Only taken me thirty years to write something you reckon has a *whiff* of Bob Blade's quality,' Dad murmurs eventually.

'So what? Now you have. Everyone gotta get lucky sometime.' Mickey's drumstick tips are against Dad's temple. Dad pushes them away.

'Now I have,' Dad mutters.

He scowls down the length of himself. 'Lookit me. Thirty years. One half-decent song, man.' Dad lights a rollie, mouth downturned, eyes slitted. 'Know how many songs Bob Blade's written the last thirty years?'

Dad stretches his arms as far as they'll go. Bulges them out. Then drops them to his lap. 'My effort dunt come close to one of his leftovers,' Dad whispers. 'Cuz no one touches him. *No one*. 'N even if my song's smokin', I'm not. *We're* not. Lookit us, man –'

While Dad throws Mickey a slow-motion, exaggerated

shrug of defeat, his hands scrunch the words and music of the song I went to the trouble of printing off for him.

Dad stands. Swaying like a man more wiped than drunk, he lobs the balled sheets one by one across the sitting room towards the bin. Misses every time.

'G'night,' he announces.

'So I'm not drummin'?' Mickey squares up to Dad. 'After you phone me out the blue? *"Had my visit from the Muse, man,"*' Mickey nails Dad perfectly. 'I no-can-doe'd a hundred and twenty quid cash-in-hand wedding gig tonight, nicked my brother's butcher's van, drove eighty miles, lugged my kit two flights without you taking a fuckin' cymbal . . .'

Getting nowhere with Dad, Mickey vents his spleen on me. 'Better do something here, junior. I'm only half-way through my anger management programme.'

'Dad?'

Slightly alarmed at the way Mickey starts shadow-boxing the space between us, I try to sound encouraging.

'Keep on truckin'.' I bob my head and smile. 'Isn't that what you tell other people when times are tough?'

But Dad just snorts then lurches towards the sitting room door.

So Mickey uses more direct action. He waddles to the far end of the room, arrowing his drumsticks at Dad's retreating head. They whistle past me en route to the base of Dad's skull. Two direct hits.

'Oi, princess. Quit fannying.'

'Whassapoint, Levon?'

'Whassapoint?' Mickey lunges after Dad before he can leave the sitting room. 'You havin' a laugh, pal?' he enquires in a voice that makes the length of my spine feel like it's been tickled with the business end of a Stanley knife.

'Don't give up now, Dad.' My own voice pipes out about two octaves higher than Mickey's. However, the fact that I produce any words at all is miraculous. Mickey, on a rage-fuelled mission to commit grievous bodily harm on Dad, full-force headbutts my ribcage when I intercept.

'Steady the buffs there, Levon. Throw one of your tantrums if you must, but I ain't singin'.' Dad ambles from the doorway to where I'm jack-knifed in the centre of the room.

'By the way, you say something to me there, Einstein?' Dad bends over so we're both side by side, eyeballing each other upside down.

'Said don't give up, Dad,' I splutter. 'Mickey's right. You need to quit fannying.'

Bloody hell! I never thought in a million years I'd find myself taking sides with Mickey. Can't honestly put my finger on why I do. Maybe Mickey knocked all the sense as well as the stuffing out of me. Or maybe, having held Dad's completed song in black and white, I figure he's embarked on something too worthwhile to abandon, and I'm not going to let him quit a job half done for once. Or maybe subconsciously I resent my mates being asked to help my dad when I never have been and I want to be part of what he's doing. Who knows? All I know for sure is that once I have my breath back, I help Mickey set up.

'Mickey's come all this way for you,' I remind Dad, slinging a guitar over his head, before he does another of his disappearing acts. At first Dad just slouches behind his mic stand, listlessly watching Mickey force two drums at once through the sitting room doorway. But moments later his left hand creeps to his fretboard. His right hand picks the strings.

'*That's* more like it, brother.' Mickey looks up from the side drums he's screwing to their stands to fix his eyes on Dad. 'Let's hear it for the new Bob Blade, eh?'

'Levon, would you ever quit calling me that? It's an insult to the man cuz there's only one Bob. And he's untouchable. Get that? You *know* that.' Dad riffs angrily through the chords of his song while he speaks. 'And I just wanna be me, Levon, but able to write like Bob. Even for fifteen minutes. Yeah.'

Dad suddenly seems sober. He's standing straight. Eyes clear.

'Yeah. Just wanna be Bob for fifteen minutes. See the world like he sees it. Then I wanna take my song to The Man. I want The Man to gimme a chance. 'Stead of taking one look. *Too old. Too ugly. Toodle-oo*.'

'What you waiting for then?'

With a soft drum roll that builds to a much heavier **duka duka DUKA duka**, Mickey nods at Dad until he's strumming hypnotically to the rhythm.

'Come on then, Fifteen Minute Bob. Sing!' I encourage Dad.

'Fifteen Minute Bob. I dig, junior!' Mickey compliments me with a drum roll as I take a seat behind the controls of Dad's eight-track. Never paid heed to the thing before, but what can be tricky about knob-twiddling? Barry and Smillie have mastered it, after all.

*

When Mum phones at midnight to yawn that no one's relieved her shift in Casualty, Mickey's so delighted he takes an impromptu drum solo that brings the looming bulk of our bouncer neighbour, Moran the Moron, to the front door.

While I'm in the hall, lending Mr Moran Dad's fancy noise reduction headphones and swearing tonight's recording session's a one-off, I can hear Mickey cackling, 'Night Nurse ain't comin' home so buckle your seatbelt, Blade man. Gunna be a long, hard ride.'

I'll say this for Mickey: gumsy troll he might be, but prison must have taught him something. He proved to be one impressive stickler.

Finicky:

'Stop chewing your words, dude.'

Nitpicking:

'My intro was late. And your bottom E's out, Blade man. We'll start over.'

We record *fourteen* versions of Dad's song – fast, faster, swampy, bluesy, folksy – with sweat progressively darkening Mickey's denim waistcoat from stone-wash to indigo before he finally twirls his sticks to the ceiling.

'That's nearer the sound we're after,' Mickey tells Dad, helping himself to a bottle of brandy from our sideboard. 'Time to get me some lovin'. See yas later,' he announces before scuttling out the flat.

I only realise we've worked till dawn when I stumble into the bathroom for a pee. Then collapse on my bed. Teeth unbrushed.

I'd have slept all day if Mum's war cry hadn't pierced me upright from my sprawl:

'Si-mon?'

Stumbled me into the hall.

'Why d'you walk out that cleaning interview, Simon? This can't go on. *I* can't go on.'

Mickey's drums was all I'm thinking. *Mum mustn't see them. She'll explode . . .*

But Mum's in the sitting room already.

'Hiya,' I call out.

'Simon, did you hear what I –' She snarls when she turns and sees me. Then she regroups. 'Rory? *Rory?*'

I'm scanning the sitting room, expecting a bombsite. Instruments everywhere. Not to mention the lingering aromas of sweat and booze and whatever it was Mickey rolled when the beer ran out. I'm too distracted by what

I *don't* find to mumble anything more than, 'Huh?'

Not so much as a cushion tassel's awry, in fact all Mum's cushions are plumped and arranged like the House Doctor's paid an out-of-hours call. *Mickey?* I gape at the empty space where we set up his drum kit. The carpet looks freshly hoovered, it's pile fluffed, and the dining room table's not only clear of the ashtrays and bottles that cluttered it last night, but it looks *polished*. Unbelievable. There isn't – I've to run my fingers along the edge of the table to check – a splinter of evidence to suggest a pumped-up drummer had been belting twelve bells out the furniture. Only the sticky-lidded bottle of Topps poking behind Dad's eight-track hints at last night's action. In the nick of time it's stuffed down my boxers. Have to do that. Because Mum's tugging me round to face her.

'Why aren't you at school? You're not sick? Where's Simon? And why's it so cold in here?'

I hesitate over Mum's quick-fire questions, mentally rehearsing the correct answers:

It's cold because Dad and Mickey were chain-smoking you know what in here. So Mickey – you remember Mickey, Mum? Went to jail for Class-A drugs offences? You hate his guts? – well, I'm guessing he cleared up and opened the window . . .

I bite my tongue, of course.

'*That's* why.' I close the windows. Checking the street outside for a butcher's van full of drums. No sign.

'And I don't know where Dad is. And I slept in.'

I shrug, keeping my back turned. And braced. Ready for another fingers-on-buzzers round: *You slept in? Why?* I only peek round when a snore breaks the silence behind me.

Mum's flat out on the settee, her head wedged between two plump cushions.

11

GOING PUBLIC

'YOU stayed up all night? Recording? Pull the other one!'

Smillie trumpets my excuse for being late even though I'm bang up next to him in the Ref, trying to shoogle on my Dinner Monitor sash without anyone noticing me. Unfortunately Selina and her pals, who happen to be sitting at the nearest table, are all ears. Damn. The way they glance out the corners of their eyes at each other, suck in their cheeks and flare their pretty nostrils is a dead giveaway.

'Oi! Baz! Guess what? Rory put drums on the song.'

Smillie, subtle as that beardie Brian Blessed actor bloke, booms the length of the table to where Barry's tucking into some kind of pudding studded with bluebottles or currants and smothered in custard.

'BAZ! BAZ!' Although Barry continues to eat steadily, Smillie's urgency has Selina and co. flicking their heads from me to the end of the table. Realising he has a dream audience, Smillie grabs my upper arms and makes them flop about before I can stiffen them.

'Hey, lookee. I'm all wasted, maaaan,' he drawls. Earns himself a giggle or two.

'Smillie, I was working –' I try to shrug free, my voice coming out all cut-up jumpy, thanks to my arm being jerked. This elicits more giggles, so I shut up. Decide to thole the humiliation. I let Smillie yank my sash up above my head till it's caught under my armpits. This allows him his moment in the limelight, pretending to be my puppet-master. Does he love that!

'Hellow, lay-deez.' I think Smillie's attempting a Barry White, walrus of love voice. 'Want me to lead you astray?' Smillie sweeps one of my hands in a circle at the girls. 'I bin up awl night long, doing baaad things.'

'Doing equations, more like,' chortles Selina, 'cuz you're *not* in a band, are you?' She scans the length of me through narrow eyes: Toes, crotch, specs, hair. '*Is* he in a band?' I catch her whispering up the table, quizzing her mates. Noticing Selina turn her back on his puppet show, Smillie quickly manoeuvres my hands till they hover above her. Then he forces them to plop on her head. Shoulders. Chest. Face.

'Oh, oh. Don't grope de lady. Bad Rory! Nawty, nawty, nawty,' Smillie squawks like Mr Punch. He stretches my arms further up the table so that I have to paw Selina's mate Amy next.

'Nawty, nawty, nawty. Touching up de laydeez like dat,' Smillie sleazes, making my arms dart randomly till all the girls are squealing. Shrinking. Recoiling. Loving it, really.

'Behave yourself there, Smiler.' Barry, his mouth ringed in custard, elbows Smillie aside. He tugs off my sash.

'Earth to Rory.' Barry's flashing a CD at me. 'What's happened here? Were you working on this?'

'Are you singing on that? Is he singing on that?' I hear Selina pipe up behind Barry. She sounds impressed though I can't see her face. Just Smillie. He's plastering a lettuce leaf off Amy's plate to his face. Spearing a tomato on to his nose.

'Me Salad Man,' he tries to entertain *les girls* with a new comedy routine, but they just ignore him. Girls mostly ignore Smillie. All eyes are watching the CD Barry's wiggling and the person he's wiggling it at. ME, in other words. *Les girls* are all looking at ME.

'*I* didn't know he was in a *band*. Coo-well,' one of

Selina's crew – Suzie, her name is – pipes up like she's suddenly noticed I exist, even though we sat next to each other for an entire year in French and I sent her a Valentine once: *Voulez vous aller à McDonald's?*

'Are you a singer . . .?' Suzie gropes about, clearly excavating my name from her 'Whatever' back-file: '. . . R–R–Ryan? Zat your CD?'

No one answers her.

Well Smillie can't. He's doing slurpy Salad Man noises, rolling his tongue about behind his lettuce skin. And Barry's homing in on me.

'What's changed about the song? Me'n'Smiler were posting it today.' It's hard to judge Barry's mood when he's wearing a custard smile, but I'm guessing he's peeved.

'*I* dunno.' I shrug. 'Dad's mate added drums. They're heavy –'

'Heavy?'

Barry's so close I smell the currants stuck to his teeth.

'How heavy? Heavy like who?'

'Not like The Who. Just heavy.'

'Like *who*?' Barry shakes me. 'Deep Purple? Led Zep? Or d'you mean Kings of the Stone Age heavy? Prog or punk or thrash or what? Ah, forget it.'

While we're talking, Barry steers me free of our intrigued audience. When he pats me kindly on the arm I feel like some kind of lost-cause.

'Don't worry yourself, Ro. Just need to hear what Bladester's changed myself.' Barry holds the CD up in front of my face. 'See, last night he was happy for us to put up this version on the interne–'

'Hey, Barry?'

'You in Rory's band too?' Like a girly backing track bursting into a song at the wrong place, Selina and her crew interrupt.

'Why didn't you say before?'

'We'll be your groupies.'

They follow me and Barry from the dinner hall, circling. Fluttering like a flitter of butterflies wanting to land. All talking at once.

'Who's singing?'

'Can we see you on the *internet*?'

'Don't be shy, Barry. You weren't shy down the basketball court.'

I can't see the look on Barry's face because the girl who's just spoken, the tallest of Selina's mates – Lauren –

she's flat up against Barry, and he's flat up against a classroom door. Sharp breathing. As they tumble through it together, he's trying to keep hold of his CD and Lauren's trying even harder to wrestle it away. But she doesn't play by WWF rules. Boy, no! One below-the-belt grope at Barry's treat-me-gentles, and our wannabe groupies are sprinting for the girls' toilets. Dad's song is in their clutches.

'Fan-bloody-brilliant.' Barry groans. 'Y'know what'll happen *now*? They'll pap that on the internet the way it is.'

'Before we've made a video. Bugger.' Salad Man scowls so hard at me, his lettuce face falls off.

'What have *I* done?' I shrug.

'Done?' Barry's incredulity makes him wince in pain. 'You're supposed to be a Superbrain, but you're so out the loop you don't think to tell your own mates how your old man's re-recording a song we said to leave with *us*. Aw, forget it, Ro. S'awright, man. No sweat. S'only music to you, I know . . .'

Barry clicks his tongue, a summons to Smillie and signal of his disappointment in me rolled into one.

12

BATHTIME FOR RORY

For the rest of the day I keep my head down. Though it's nothing to do with Barry limping off all huffy-puffy with me, or Smillie reminding me how, for a good mate, I'm 'well weird sometimes. For real.'

'I'll remember that, Oliver. For real.' Calling Smillie by his first name repays his dig tenfold. The stricken look of shame I bring to his face keeps me chuckling all the way to double Physics.

'Going to be in your *element* today,' Doc Martin welcomes me, all chuckles himself. He's flourishing a brace of exam papers. One for me. One for Annette Muir who's Doc's only other pupil and who needs to scrape a pass in Physics to be considered for the uni course she fancies. Poor Annette, between you and me, and pretty damn fine as she is, she's *not* in her element like I am. The girl's dire at Physics. I know, because I redo all her homework before she hands it in, and she's yet to produce a single correct answer off her own bat. Beats me why she doesn't just pick another uni that doesn't want Physics and quit Doc Martin's class. Five hours a week she sits behind me, gasping '*Ooos*' of panic whenever he asks her a question.

So this afternoon, while I'm nestled in my comfort zone, Thermal Expansion calculations practically scribbling themselves, Annette spends the double period sighing. Sighing so hard behind me, her breath tickles the hairs on the back of my neck. Hot at first. Then shivery cold.

Not an entirely unpleasant sensation I admit to myself as Doc announces, 'All good things must come to an end,' and bumbles over to take my paper away.

Ahhhhhh. Finally I release a long sigh myself. Though one of satisfaction because I genuinely can't recall spending an hour feeling so damn *good*. My body feels a bit like it's been steeped in a long, deep bath. Not that I have all that many, by the way. Just now and again I take a notion, and I love the way when you come out and swaddle up in a towel, every limb weighs heavy and slow.

Deliciously heavy and slow, I confess, feeling ever so guilty at my own contentment when I squinch round and read Annette's pale despair.

'Tough?' I mouth.

Annette shrugs me a double thumbs down. She exhales another of her sighs. This one hits my face full on.

Hot at first.

Then shivery cold.

And while this is happening, her breath seems to freeze the air hanging in the space between us. And for the first time in the weeks I've known her, I find myself gazing properly deep into her eyes.

They're silvery-grey. And really beautiful. Softer than Selina's. Much softer, I'm realising, aware of my own eyes widening, locking on Annette's, unable to switch focus. I must be smiling or frowning, or doing something unusual with my features because Annette's cheeks suddenly flare as livid as tinned salmon.

'What? You're staring.' She shoves her Physics folder up to her face, her chair legs raking the floor as she hurries to leave the room. 'Oo, by the way, heard Selina playing your song in the toilets. S'great,' she mumbles from the doorway.

'Annette, wait. Nettie. It's not my song.' Like I've never used her name before, I test it in the empty room.

'Nettie.'

My heart is beating so fast and so loud, you'd think Mickey had muscled his way under my ribcage.

13
SIRENS

Realising you really fancy someone can be pretty dangerous. Following my pulse-quickening experience with 'Nettie', as I've decided to secretly call her, I loiter the corridors in the vain hope of 'bumping' into her again.

'Did you manage any of the Physics questions?' I plan to silver-tongue devil her. Alas, she's already offski, and by following the tattoo of my foolish heart, I arrive late at the bus shelter.

'Bollocks. Should've just walked three miles in the rain,' I groan when I clock the squealy, pealy harpy-crush gathered in the shelter. Too late though.

'Come in out the wet.'

'Plenty room, Rory.'

'We don't bite.'

Soon as they see me, Selina and Suzie and Lauren hoik me into the shelter. Me, who up till lunchtime was of less interest to these girls than a bargain rail of last year's jeans.

'It's dry,' the girls circle and purr.

'We'll look after you,' Selina promises.

Bet you will, I gulp, recalling the state of Barry and Smillie after they succumbed to the Sirens one day when it snowed and the bus never came and I walked and they didn't.

Lip gloss. That's what Barry was wearing when he escaped. Lucky for me the bus appears before Lauren waxes my eyebrows or something.

'Buussssssss!'

Honestly, the sight of those females stampeding the crammed vehicle instead of waiting twenty minutes for the next! These Sirens are Neanderthal.

Needless to say, I'm the last passenger squeezed aboard. I stay up front, close to the driver.

'Freeze your veins, that lot,' the driver shudders.

'Too right, mate,' I agree, pulling the bottom of my shirt from my trousers to wipe the steam off my specs. Is *that* short-sighted of me?

'Phoar. Whip 'em all off! Come and give us a lap dance!' Lauren's gruff voice chimes.

'Let it all hang out.'

This time the voice is closer. Whoever speaks triggers a ripple of whoops throughout the bottom deck. Then a chant begins:

Un-button.

Un-button.

'Ooooh! So there's more to you than brains, Rory.'

This comment, I realise, daring to glance round, emanates from Selina. Perched on Suzie's knee, she's waggling a personal CD player in my direction. Her skirt is hitched so far up her thigh, my specs steam up all over again.

'Got your song here. Lovin' it,' Selina simpers, making sure her tongue deliberately lingers on the 'l' of love. 'But it sounds rubbish on this machine. Listen.'

Just and no more, over the swish of the bus through the rain, a tinny *ticka-ticka-ticka* dribbles from the headphones Selina holds to my ear.

'But you could just sing the song live. Right here on the bus. Give us a concert.'

'Yeah. Do it. And we'll join in. A-three. A-two. A-one –' To my horror, Lauren is stormtroopering up the bus towards me, her arms sweeping giant circles round her head. 'Yeah. C'mon. Give us a show. ". . . *The story, of my, story of my, story of my* . . ."' She grabs my arms and shakes me.

'For God's sake. It's *your* bloody song. Sing!' She shakes me harder.

'Gonna let us off here, mate?' I implore the bus driver, even though I'm still two long, wet miles from home.

14
BRAIN DAMAGED BY BLADE

Not only am I soaked when I reach the flat, but I'm shivering. And not just because my shirt is wet, and my trousers are clinging to me, and my numb toes squelch in my shoes. No. I'm shivering at the memory of . . .

Those females!!!

Inviting me to unbutton my shirt!!!!!!

Just because they think ***I've*** *written a daft song.*

'Puh!' I squeeze my trousers out over the bath. 'It's changed *everything,* that song,' I splutter. And the exact same moment *I'm* talking, these Bob Blade lyrics scatter-gun through my head. I'm hearing a mocking mash-up, about times bein' outa joint and whack' – whatever that means – and strange things . . . 'goin' down right and left. Strange things I sure can't comprehend.'

Arggg! How come Bob Blade's songs can just pop into

my consciousness like that – boo! – when the guy means *nothing* to me? Why should his lyrics revolve in my head? Like a scratchy old LP with the needle stuck. Giving me brain damage.

'And anyway, I *do* comprehend what's happening, actually, Mr Blade!'

Only by barking over my uninvited brain-guest in my point-of-information voice can I shut him up.

'Those girls think I want to be a singer. Come on: I'd sooner agree to marry one of them, than try a caper like that for goodness' sakes.'

I don't believe this. I'm muttering away to my myself again – sneerily, Bob Blade-ily – as I thud into my room. Minus trousers and underpants, I should add.

Well it's not like I'm *expecting* Barry and Smillie to be plonked on my bed. But there they are. I've to fumble about for dry boxers while the pair of them freeze in suspended animation, goggling my privates. It's only when I'm decent that I notice Barry's holding my big 35mm camera, and Smillie's balancing my teddy on his head.

'Christ, Rory! Quit dangling,' Smillie tuts, covering Mr Cuddles' eyes.

And yes, okay, I still have a teddy. Obviously not in *bed* with me any more. But I still keep Mr Cuddles. So? We go back a long way. It's not like he's *hurting* anyone.

In fact, the only creature being hurt *is* Mr Cuddles. Smillie's using him to whack me about. 'We've been waiting ages,' he complains, swinging poor Mr Cuddles by the leg in the space between him and Barry.

'But you're here now, Ro.'

At least Barry has the grace to look sheepish.

'Bladester said we were fine hanging here while he nipped out on business,' he shrugs. Then changes the subject.

'Why were you chuntering about girls annoying you? And mimicking Bob Blade's voice out there. D'you often do that in the nip?'

Oh man. I can only cringe at Barry's 'Gotcha' grin.

'Actually, I'm only stripped because I was soaked after Selina and her pals pulled me into the bus shelter . . .'

'What?'

'Go on, Ro!'

Bingo!

Honestly, for the next five minutes I feel like Sir Ian McGandalf reading The Chronicles of Narnia on *Jackanory*.

Neither Barry nor Smillie blink. They just watch my mouth moving. Transfixed.

Jackanory-time over, Barry is first to react. 'So the girls all think it's you singing?' He's nodding while he speaks. Approvingly.

'Hear that? The chicks all think it's *Rory* on the CD.'

Now Smillie's nodding in time with Barry. They're both smirking.

'Very, *very* interesting, Barry.'

Interesting?

Interesting?

I was expecting a little more in the line of sympathy from Barry, at least, but he's not even looking at me now. He's bent over my camera. Pom-pomming Dad's tune.

'Guys, it *was* really scary with those girls –' I'm still seeking mate-support, but only Smillie appears to be listening.

'Sexy scary.' He writhes about on my bed like there's a ferret nipping his treat-me-gentles. 'You've just missed the ride of your life.'

Puh-lease! I'm distinctly uncomfortable about the way Smillie's arranging Mr Cuddles on his thigh to recreate how hot Selina looked on Suzie's knee.

I should never have included that detail.

'Could you see right up Selina's skirt? Could you clock her frillies? Bet they were red.' Smillie jiggles Mr Cuddles in anticipation of titbits there's no way I'm supplying. (Even though the answers are: 1.Yes. 2. Yes. 3.Green.)

'Calm down.' Barry slings poor teddy into a corner. 'We're working here, Smiler. Hold it –' He nudges Smillie off my bed and shoots a picture of me without looking into the viewfinder.

''S'not a toy, that,' I say. 'And you need the lens cap off to take photos.'

''*S'not a toy,*' Barry wheedles, then he turns the camera over in his hands. Grumps, 'Whozza lens cap?'

'Just tell us and pose.' Smillie pings the elastic on my boxers. 'Imagine you're seeing up Selina's skirt –'

That does it.

'I've homework.' I open my door.

Neither Barry nor Smillie budge. They do look up and beam, though.

Only because Dad's sweeping into the bedroom, patting my backside on his way past.

'Howdy doody. Sorry, no way, Einstein –'

Scrunching his face like someone's just let one go,

Dad zig-zags the two fingers holding his cig the length of my torso.

'– that is *not* the image we're after, lads,' he purses.

I don't believe this. Having my mates invade my room is one thing, but now Dad is lolled across my bed too, blowing smoke rings at the ceiling, and dropping fag ash on my duvet.

'Whose idea was it to snap Wonderboy nude? Don't work. Sorry.' He plucks my camera from Barry's grasp. 'Still, you've figured what you're doing with this box of tricks now?' he asks Barry.

Not me.

President of St Bernard's Photographic Club.

Winner, with my 'Seagull. Chip. Fight' of our District News picture competition. The press clipping of me collecting my book token prize from our local MP is literally hanging above Dad's head. And he's consulting *Barry* about photography.

'Barry doesn't have a *clue*.' Snatching my camera back I make a show of releasing the lens cap. 'You can't just point and shoot with this. You need flash, and it takes batteries. I keep mine out the camera in case they leak. Voilà . . .'

With no disrespect to Mr Cuddles, whose loyal, furry,

upside-down face is fixed on mine throughout this impromptu photography lesson, I'm dismayed to find I'm yakking to myself: 'Oi! Thought you were taking pictures . . .?'

Then I hear Dad, Barry and Smillie hurrying down the stairs.

'We'll use my digital for pics instead.' Barry's voice echoes up two landings. 'Less faffing. Quality should be fine.'

'S'long as it's easy to whack on the web.' Smillie's voice overlaps.

'Those science prof specs need to come off him first,' Dad snorts.

'And clothes *on*,' Smillie chips in. '*We* didn't tell Ro to strip. He just burst in –'

'Singin',' Barry adds.

'Einstein singin'? Christ! Sorry I missed that –'

A chummy guffaw billows up to where I'm standing.

'*What planet did you spring from, little bitty son of mine?*' Dad's croon swirls through the stairwell. Alone, in my pants, I lean over the banister.

'Strange things are going down right enough,' I sigh to myself.

15
STEALING MY SOUL

'You don't know where Simon went?'

It's hours since Dad disappeared with my mates. Two since Mum came home. Told me she was so knackered, she conked out on a spare trolley during a Dressing clinic.

'Manager's given me written warning. Perfect!'

Mum keeps worrying the cottage pie grown cold between us. She slivers potato mash from the portion she's keeping for Dad.

'Went to do something about a camera.' I hesitate before adding. 'With Barry and Smillie.' *They didn't tell me what.*

'And they didn't tell you what?' Mum's eyes lock on mine. She drills a reading.

'Simon better not be *buying* any cameras.'

Mum lifts a spoonful of Dad's cottage pie to her mouth. Before it reaches her lips she slops it back into the dish. Carefully, like she's shaping the sides of a sandcastle, she blocks and pats Dad's dinner into a neat square. Then she smooshes it to mush.

'I'm done in,' she barely whispers. 'Too weary for Simon and his shenanigans.' Mum runs the flat of her hand across her forehead, like she's trying to iron out her worries. 'And listen to me, giving out to you, pet. Sorry,' she sighs, rising as the phone rings in the hall.

'Sister Ryan. Ward Nine,' I hear Mum answer robotically. Before she realises her mistake, or that the voice down the line is the same one singing into her other ear, Dad is waltzing her back into the kitchen.

'*You keep my heart a-beatin'*,' he croons, cradling a fancy-looking mobile phone as if it's a microphone.

'*You set my pulse on fire –*'

Dad coils himself round Mum. '*Hot sister Ria,*' His lips close on hers.

'*My only, my desire.*'

Dad's lips barely graze Mum's and she's pushing him off. 'What's this?' She snatches the mobile. Shakes it like she expects it to ring her with an explanation.

'A golden ticket.' Dad makes an *abracadabra* flourish, plucking the mobile from Mum, then spinning round to catch me unawares. Whipping my specs off, he snaps a photograph.

'Don't look so *cwoss*, Einstein.'

Dad makes a pantomime of using the tip of his pinkie finger to delete the image.

'Smile this time, sweetie.' He struts around me, hand on hip, pouting Mick Jagger-ishly. Clicks picture after picture while I frown even harder.

'Where d'that phone come from, Dad?'

'And how did you pay for it, Simon?'

Mum doesn't sound as ratty as I do. Just anxious.

'Dad?' I'm dodging the eye in his phone. 'How much?'

'We're really broke, Simon.'

This time, I catch the strain in Mum's voice.

'Simon, I'm talking to you!'

'*Dad*.'

'Told you,' Dad continues clicking. 'This way. Last time,' he sing-songs. Then finally lays the mobile across both palms before presenting it to Mum.

'I told you both,' he says patiently, 'but you never list-*en*: this is the golden ticket. And –uh-uh, my righteous angel –' Dad raises a nicotine-stained finger as Mum tries to interrupt. 'It cost nothin'.'

'So you stole a *phone*, Simon?'

'Ria!' Dad punches a wounded fist to his chest.

'Well you smuggled all my daddy's Clancy Brothers records out of Ireland,' Mum snaps back. 'Not asking's stealing in my book.'

'Ach, your old fella was none the wiser – woulda needed an ear trumpet to hear them,' Dad swats away Mum's accusation. 'Anyway, Bob Blade always borrowed records without asking –'

'Stole,' Mum and I chorus.

'You're calling Bob Blade a *thief* –'

'Simon, I'm not calling him anything. Don't care if he's a feckin' axe murderer,' Mum hisses through clenched teeth. '*He* doesn't live here. And *he* isn't permanently out of work, sending his wife demented –'

Mum's downturned mouth drives a slump into Dad's shoulders. Curves a droop in his neck.

'Simon, I'm sorry . . .' Mum's voice quavers. She lays her hand on Dad's arm. '. . . you're not a bad man, and I know you still dream of making it with your music, but the reality . . .' As she sighs, Mum lifts her arm away again. Sweeps it round the room. 'I'm just about through. With everything. You.'

Ouch.

How can words be said so quietly yet make such an impact? Suddenly everything seems to hang a little looser on Dad than it did when he swaggered in flashing the mobile. 'Didn't steal no phone, Ria. Didn't buy one, neither.' Dad shrugs. Tries to muster a smile. 'But I've just sold a couple. Down the pub. Found me a sideline. Like you wanted.'

Dad dips his hands into his pockets as he speaks. Fishes out about a dozen phones. All shapes and sizes.

'You call stealin' a crime? Here's a crime of the times – hey that sounds like a Bob Blade title: *Crime o' the Times* –' Dad breaks off from what he's saying to gaze into a corner of the kitchen ceiling. '*Crime o' the times . . .*' he rasps down his nose. 'Yeah. *Crime o' the times. Talkin' grown cheap . . .*' He focuses on Mum again. 'And I'm gonna profit from it. Twenty quid already. See?' Dad clatters a handful of coins on the table.

'That's *eight* quid.' I do a quick spot of mental arithmetic.

'Can't a working man buy himself a drink with his own wages? Sheesh!'

Dad adds a couple more phones to the pile.

'Look. Unwanted upgrades. Didn't nick me nothin'.' Dad's fishing for the camera-phone again. He shows Mum a gurning snap of Barry and Smillie.

'Einstein's compadres have drawerfuls of these babies lying around on their arses doing nothing.'

'Lying about on their arses doing nothing, eh?' I mutter. Glance from Dad to Mum. *Is she thinking what I'm thinking?*

'Their old fellas get sent upgrades. Whole piles for their staff. Hardly anyone bothers swapping. So, my Lady of the Lamp,' Dad takes a very unflattering snap of Mum with her eyebrows practically scrunched to her nose, 'I'm only selling on one man's junk. Gonna keep this though.' Dad holds up the phone he's been using. 'Just for snaps. Doesn't have a SIN card –'

Before I can correct Dad's technological blooper, Mum cuts in.

'But what d'you need any *camera* for, Simon? To photograph your life passing before your eyes?'

Mum slams the kitchen door so hard on her way out the kitchen, three mugs fall from their hooks and smash. 'Punting phones won't pay our rent.' Her final words ring through the hall.

'But, Ria, this is a *sideline*. I've seen through the hazy lookin'-glass, too,' Dad calls after Mum. He's being deadly serious, by the way.

'Course you have,' I sneer into Dad's viewfinder before clamping my hand over it.

'You never steal, eh?' I push the phone away. 'Then why've you been stealing my soul since you came home?'

'Told you. This is the golden ticket. *A change is gonna come,*' Dad sings. 'Sam Cooke wrote that. Not Bob Blade. Sounds like Bob, though. Dunnit?' he witters to himself, still stealing my soul.

16
HEAVY WEATHER

So, here we are. Another happy family night chez Ryan. Dad's in his den, duetting with Bob through *Bleedin' Acid from the Soul,* his favourite Bob Blade album. ('That folk claim was born from the poor cat's crumbling marriage. Like it matters. It's a masterpiece whatever,' so Dad's lectured me since I was in Pampers.) Crooning away, Dad sounds contented enough, yet there's this dark cloud hanging over the flat: Eggy. Unshifting. Mum's mood, of course, is the prevailing source of low pressure. Yet ever since she smashed those mugs, her door's been shut tight. Not a peep from behind it.

Mum's silence isn't silent silence though. It's toxic noise. Ear-splitting.

How come couples can do that? Fight without a word being exchanged? Radiate thoughts so grim, you *smell* them?

I don't think I've ever felt so edgy, trying to ignore

Mum's unhappiness, even though it's seeping under my door and swirling round me. Clinging. It's horrible, knowing my mum's wretched and *all* I can do about it is study. Try my best.

After all, it's not *me* she's raging with.

As Dad passes my door to answer the phone which sits just outside – 'Hey dude, how's it hanging?' he has the cheek to fricking *hum* like everything's hunky dory.

Hearing Dad so chipper, I'm actually tempted to lamp him:

Mum's gonna leave us if you don't shape up.

But there's no way I can interfere. That would be IT. Mum'd detonate if she caught me offering marriage guidance to Dad on her behalf. So I stay put. Make an effort to focus on my Maths notebook, swallowing the urge to bawl Dad out for rabbitting too loud with whoever's on the other end of our line: *'D'you mind? Some of us are trying to work.'*

Comments like that are reflex with me. Even though – shh, don't tell Dad – normally any noise he makes doesn't *actually* bother me. In fact, I'm so used to having Dad singing, or the real Bladester wheezing and jingle-jangling, I reckon the pair of them subconsciously aid my concentration. You know, like Bach and Mozart are meant to do.

Why the hell then, do I hassle old daddy Blade for no reason?

The truth?:

I don't know.

Maybe I'm just proving – proving to myself and to Mum – that I'm *nothing* like the man.

And what a hypocrite I'd be tonight if I burst out and accused Dad of disturbing my studies. I've given up on working, too busy earwigging his conversation instead.

Who's he talking to?

About USB cables: 'Dude, what's a port? Ain't that what I told you to drink with brandy when you're hungover?'

About loading photographs: 'Say what? I link the *phone* up to the computer . . .? *This* phone?'

During Dad's conversation, he has to keep dumping our receiver down on the hall table – 'Oh, man, lemme go see if I can do what you're tellin' me . . .' – to dash off to the computer. That's because us Ryans are the only saddos in the civilised world with a single phone jack for their landline. It's connected to a dial-with-your-fingers handset which Barry and Smillie think is hilarious. Oh, how they love braying into the mouthpiece like posh twits from some 1920s' Murder Mystery: Chin chin. Toodle pip. Course, they don't have to *live* full-time with the inconvenience of a non-walkabout phone. It's a nightmare, as Dad's discovering once he's sprinted from the hall to the computer a dozen times. After about five minutes, the exertion of dashing back and forth, listening to instructions and carrying them out, catches up with him. From behind my bedroom door I catch the faint rasp of him sparking up a rollie. Then the creak of the sofa.

'Breather, man,' he pecks. 'Time out.'

While he's busy wheezing away in the sitting room like a pair of bellows with emphysema, I creep into the hall. Pick up the phone.

'Hey, man?' I drawl in my best stoner-dad voice.

'OK. Right. You've clicked on MENU. So now go to –' Barry's familiar voice greets me down the line.

Unfortunately I miss the rest of his instruction because Dad opens the sitting room door and I have scoot back to my bedroom before he catches me.

'Error, man. The screen's all black and trippy. Lemme call you back.' Dad's farewell lament to Barry camouflages the creak of my door closing. Phew, just in time too, because Dad's standing right outside. His studded belt rakes the woodwork as the shadow of his backside sliding to the carpet breaks the stripe of light seeping from the hall.

'Technology's screwing me, man,' Dad groans and he's so close to me I'm surprised he doesn't hear the thoughts I'm pulsing out: *'Oi! Ask **me** for help then!'*

But that would just make life too normal, wouldn't it? A father and son putting their heads together. Apart from last night's all-night one-off blip which only happened because Mickey was on hand to referee, we've not done that since I was four and Dad tried to teach me how to play Bob Blade's kid reggae song 'What Kinda Cheese is the Moon?' on the guitar. But I couldn't shape a single chord. Gave up instead. Lost it. Bubbled that making music was a stupid thing to do anyway. Counting was much, much better fun . . .

Anyway, here's Dad on his side of the door. Me on the other, forehead pressed into it. I'm trying not to breathe too loud. Trying not to think about my specs. How they're slipping down my nose. Just on the point of driving me insane when Dad's bones crack loudly. His shadow moves away.

The front door closes.

And Dad's footsteps become a fading echo on the stairs.

I'm straight on to the computer. First I yank out the USB cable Dad's forced into the wrong port. His fancy mobile is attached to the other end, a scowling photo of me set as wallpaper. What a pie I look, specs squint and eyes popping like I'm getting my prostate fingered. I delete myself. Go talk to Barry on the phone again. As myself this time.

'What's going on here? Just tell me, right?' I'm practising while I dial. Unfortunately a voice three octaves higher than Barry's answers, 'Masterton Residencia,' and I'm stuck with 'Call me Ginny, sweetheart' moaning about how the *terrible* rain's been playing havoc with her golf handicap.

'By the way, sweetheart,' Mrs M tells me just as I'm losing the will to live, 'Barry's out helping Oliver with something computery-wootery. I didn't even know it was one of Barry's subjects.'

It's not, I nearly blurt. But I'd never get off the line. And Smillie's my next phone-a-friend.

'Doing something technical at Barry's. Staying over,' Smillie's dippy mum drawls. She suggests I send 'Ollie' a message in my head. 'You've such a strong friendship, he'll sense you need him.'

I stick to calling Smillie's mobile. His voicemail clicks on: *'Hey baby, talk dirty enough an' I'll call ya back.'* (Good thing mumsy prefers telepathy and never rings her 'Ollie', eh?) Barry's mobile's the same. Non-porn message, naturally, but voicemail. Pair of them off the radar.

Odd.

And very frustrating. All I can do is my press-ups and my packed lunch (peanut butter and Marmite). It could almost be a normal school-night bedtime . . . if it wasn't for the lingering bad atmosphere in the flat.

The absence of chat from Mum.

The silence from Dad's guitar.

All I hear as I go about my business is that mesmerising hook from Dad's song. It's jammed on permanent rotation in my head:

Stor-ee of my, Stor-ee of my

Stor-ee of my life . . .

17
STRANGE NIGHT, STRANGER DAYS

Have I mentioned yet that I need earplugs in bed?

Big deal *I* say, though Barry and Smillie find this eccentricity more hilarious than my toodle-pip phone. Of course, they don't know my earplug attachment stems from when us Ryans lived in a London bedsit. Being only a toddler, I can't remember it, but Mum does: 'One room. Shared toilet. Cockroaches. Hell.'

Her and Dad were at rock bottom. The good old days, eh? Dad was busking theatre queues with Mickey. Mickey dealing and fencing gear. Dad kept bringing monged pond-life home to score while Mum worked any shifts going. She says Dad's hangers-on freaked me so much I stopped sleeping. Hence the earplugs. Apart from Social Services, it was all Mum could think of. Or afford.

And they worked. So well I can't sleep without them

now. They're that security blanket thing you need for a good night's kip . . . well, that security blanket thing *I* need: Earplugs and Mr Cuddles, who arrived on the scene about the same time.

I'm only mentioning the earplugs, by the way, because they're to blame for the shock I experience this morning after last night, when Barry and Smillie seemed to be uncontactable . . .

They're contactable now. I crush Smillie's head on my way to the bathroom. What a vile way to start a new day. Sticking your toes in somebody's wet morning-mouth. Smillie is not amused either.

But how was I to know he was kipping on my floor? I was out for the count, busy experiencing curious, lifelike half-dreams where 'Story of My Life' kept playing beyond my earplugs, while voices whispered around my face and sniggers were stifled and flashes of light made me roll across the pillow to a dimmer side of the mattress . . .

It wasn't like I'd *invited* Smillie to stay. Or Barry. But there *he* is too, materialising from my steamy bathroom like a contestant from *Stars in Your Eyes*.

'All yours, Ro,' Barry waves me towards my own

shower like *I'm* the surprise visitor here.

Waves me – since Barry doesn't grasp the concept of rationed hot water – towards a Baltic shower. I suppose economy's not an issue when your house has six bathrooms.

'Oi! Wh–what's going on?' I chitter at Barry, but he's drifted off, taking the towel with him, of course.

Smillie doesn't tell me what's going on either. By the time I drip from the shower he's under my duvet farting and groaning with pride at his own smells. Till Barry grabs his feet.

'Aw, stop gassing Rory's mattress. He's to sleep there tonight. Get up. Bladester's waiting.' He drags Smillie past me, only pausing to shudder at the vision of me naked.

'Y'mind, Ro? Saw enough of that yesterday, and I've not had breakfast yet.'

'Poor you!' I sark after Barry, dressing as quickly as it's possible when you've towelled off with a T-shirt. The kitchen's like the *Marie Celeste* when I go to join Barry and Smillie.

That's inaccurate.

There was food in the kitchen of the *Marie Celeste*. Not just dirty cereal bowls and spilled milk. A note from Mum:

Have a good day, Rory.
Will food-shop after work.
Sorry for last night!!!!
Not your fault.

Stomping into the sitting room, I lob the scrunched wrapper I found in the breadbin at Barry and Smillie. The pair of them, plus Dad, are hunched over the computer, munching toast from a piled plate. None of them so much as glance in my direction. Dad's song is playing. The Mickey version I helped produce.

'This is cracking. And the more you hear it, the better it sounds –'

Spookily echoing my own thoughts, Barry bunches

his fingers to his lips. Kisses them open. For a second he catches my eye. 'S'crackin',' his mouth and head jerk down in synchronised approval. Approval that includes me. Fleetingly. Before Barry nudges Dad. 'But our promo's gonna make it stellar. Forget punting mobiles –'

'Yeah, Superstar, our promo's gonna make it stellar –'

Smillie's parroted interruption gobs toast all over the computer.

'Aw, minger!' I lunge at the monitor to swipe it clean. Only I trip. Break my fall on the keyboard.

ERROR . . .

ERROR . . .

ERROR . . .

Bleeps the screen, instantly blue-blank beneath the flashing warning. The monitor's eeking the kind of noise you hear on hospital soaps when someone pegs it. High-pitched. Panic-stricken.

ERROR . . .

ERROR . . .

I don't believe this!

While this is happening on the computer, the same high-pitched note starts bleeping in my head.

And not just because Smillie's face snarls so close to

mine, I can tell the jam sticking to his molars is apricot.

And not just because Barry's cheeks, as he falsettos, 'What have you done there, Ro?' and gesticulates from me to the blue screen, have turned as hypertensive beetroot as his old man's.

And not just because Dad's slumped over the keyboard, both fists thudding his temples like he's channelling the spirit of Mickey.

These three extreme reactions are only partly responsible for the way my brain eeks and bleeps. Mainly it's trying to process something I caught on the monitor before it died:

Images of ME.

flashing and dotting over the screen –

Me smiling

Me frowning

Specs on

Specs off

Me pouting

Me sleeping

Eyes open

Eyes closed

Hair ruffled

Hair combed

Side parting

Side on

Me

Me

Me . . .

The appearance and disappearance of each me was syncopated to Dad's song. Against the backdrop of a guitarist in silhouette. Skinny. Jiving. He could be me too.

Or he could be Dad. Impossible to tell.

'Oi. What's with these pictures?'

'Did you guys *film* me last night?'

'Please talk to me? I need to go to school . . .'

'Wish you would, Einstein,' Dad growls. He's rummaging the drawer where Mum stuffs instruction leaflets, most of which have outlived their respective gadgetry: An electric knife, a foot spa (Mum's Christmas from me one year), cheapo hair straighteners (Dad's Christmas to himself when he went temporarily Emo . . .)

'You've done enough damage,' Dad chucks a brochure

about Vancouver over his shoulder. Then an Allen key and a bag of screws, attached to an IKEA diagram.

As he's speaking, Barry and Smillie stare at me.

ERROR . . .

ERROR . . .

ERROR . . . is flashing in mirror writing on their blank faces, their blue-tinged stares spookily mesmerising. If I didn't know how poncy they insist Drama is, I'd be tempted to accuse my mates of *acting* zombie. Only to wind me up. After all, deleting data in Computing is something they routinely do for 'shits and giggles'.

But neither of them are giggling now. From the way they gawp at the monitor, it looks like they're regretting the attention they paid boobsnbutts.com in First Year while I was earning my A* in Recovery Strategies.

It's lucky for them Data Retrieval is a piece of cake. While Dad's keening, 'Do I look up "Meltdown", man?' and flipping the index of the bible-sized manual to some PC we dumped donkey's ago, the first bar of his song is already jangling.

Not that anyone throws me a *merci*.

Not even when I gasp, 'Hey look!' as the monitor colour-changes from blue to black to sepia-tinted. On screen is a close-up image of a tapping pointy-leather toecap.

'Look, Dad! Those boots! You're wearing them!' I exclaim, thought not, by the way, to garner even a smidge of praise for this *video* file I've only dredged from cyber-limbo. I exclaim because I'm *genuinely* excited to see Dad shod in these Fancy Dan boots some cowgirl bought him a long time ago in the Nashville Boot Store.

Nashville, Tennessee, that is.

According to Ryan-lore, this happened when Dad, officially renamed Blade, and having broken his mother's heart, returned to the States to ride box cars and pen mournful ditties. Dad's always been somewhat hazy about what he actually got up to while he was meant to be wandering the Lost Highway like a hobo, but according to Mum, he mostly lived the high life with some heiress who spotted him puzzling over a fistful of dollars at Mobile Airport. Decided to take him under her wing.

But I've always known about the cowboy boots.

These fancy cowboy boots have lived so long top of Dad's wardrobe, their box is thatched with dust. Mum thinks they're ridiculous.

Maybe they are. A bit. But they're beautiful. Charcoal and cream. Handmade. Even though it must be ten years since a tipsy Dad on childminding duty last allowed me to rub the dappled hide between my fingers and thumb, I still recall the buttery feel of them. Their rich smell. Remember Dad putting his arm round me and whispering, 'Juz you wait, Rory. Thesh dudes'll take the spotlight one day. Whena time comes.'

'Whena time comes . . . wow!' Recalling Dad's words, with a little shiver of excitement, and also remembering the feeling of his arm slung round my shoulder, I edge between Barry and Smillie at the computer. But before my backside makes contact with a chair, the screen's flicked to blank.

'Best you get offski, Einstein.'

Dad barely murmurs. Just cocks his head towards the sitting room door.

On either side of Dad, Barry and Smillie hold themselves rigid. Pair of them the epitome of Cringe.

'You want me to leave?' I ask, wishing my mates would look me in the eye.

'You heard.' Dad leans over Barry. 'Shut it all down, man,' he tells him, waiting till Barry's obeyed with a sigh before he turns back to me. 'Mum won't like you missing schoolly-woolly.'

'Aren't you guys coming with me?'

I dodge round Dad.

'Hey!' I grip Barry's shoulder, trying to force him to look me in the eye.

'Look, Ro.' I feel his muscles contract under my hand. Shrink. 'We'll just finish up what we've started here. Catch you later, OK?'

Barry's eyes *almost* meet mine when Dad steps between us so we're chest to chest.

'You're all right, man,' Dad tells my mate. I can count the frill of liner-smudged wrinkles round Dad's eyes, their tally doubling as he narrows his gaze.

'Away split the atom, Rory,' Dad's mouth twists like something tastes sour. 'S'not like you've ever been into my bag, man.'

The other night. We worked together. It was great – I'm almost tempted to cut in, but the tension between me and Dad crackles electric. Dangerous. So I do as I'm told and leave the flat.

18

HELLO WORLD

The morning's cold. Gusty. Pissing wet. My mood doesn't improve when my bus swings round a corner while I'm chasing it down.

Perfect.

'Sorry, Mrs Stanton.'

Late for Maths, specs opaque with rain and condensation, I burble to the moving outline at the front of the class. I could be talking to a filing cabinet for all I know. Alas, I'm not.

'Oh. My. God! Are you *trying* to be funny?'

When Selina rasps at the fatal insult I've paid her in front of the *whole* class, the temperature of icy rain trickling off the ends of my hair instantly soars. I'm giving off steam as I lift my specs.

'You thought I was Stat? Tosser.' Selina doesn't actually hiss these words, but her eyes do.

'Sit down and stop disrupting my lesson again,' the

genuine Stat snaps from where she's looming over Nettie, slashing red lines through her workbook. Even without my specs on I can see how fiercely Nettie's blushing.

Blushing pretty fiercely myself, I squelch to the back of the room. While I hold my specs to the window, using my tie to dry them, I spot two blurry shapes puddle-stomping under a massive red golf brolly. MASTERTON CONSTRUCTION it's emblazoned bold enough for me to read spec-less. Glasses back on, I watch Smillie jack-knife, slapping his thighs at something Barry says. Even through glass, my mates' guffaws reach my ears.

Wonder if they're concocting today's excuse for swanning in late first period? I coulda pretended my bus was hijacked too. Or something. Just once, if Dad'd let me stay, I wince, dangerously close to self-pity. Then I hear Mum's voice in my head.

'Find a silver lining instead of feeling sorry for yourself.'

And Mum's right, as usual. *Stat's let me off the hook for being late. No detention.* I cheer up a little, though I soon realise that she's not just leaving me be. She's ignoring me.

Because I'm the only pupil to volunteer, 'Misssss!' when she challenges, 'Who can simplify problem three?'

'Nobody?' Stat's gaze sweeps the class. 'Selina? Alistair? Annette? Come *on*, Annette, *try* for once,' she hectors.

'Missssss!!!' I'm almost out my seat trying to catch at least one of Stat's eyes. I raise my voice too, but only Nettie pays attention. She keeks over her shoulder. Darts me a shrug-cum-smile-cum-blush. Actually, strike that. Nettie's the only person who looks *round*. *Acknowledges* she hears me. But *everyone* is paying attention.

You know how you *know* when people are all ears? From the set of their backs.

'Ach, forget it, Miss.'

When I blurt my frustration aloud, there's a collective gasp of surprise. It's followed by an outbreak of snuffling and coughing into sleeves.

'Did somebody speak?' A humourless smile plays on Stat's face as she pretends to fix on someone she can't see. I don't rise to the bait and for the rest of the lesson I zone into the workbook on my desk.

Or so it would seem to the casual observer: You'd swear I'm oblivious to the sidelong evils Selina throws me every time she flicks her hair. Or deaf to Stat's invitation to, 'Stop writing,' while she explains another tricky calculation Nettie's messed up. Towards the end of the lesson you'd think also I'd missed a simultaneous text received on everyone's phone.

But check me out closer. Under the camouflage of my knitted brows, I clock a dozen hands slipping into vibrating trouser pockets. Oh yes.

And I notice how every thumb opens a text before screens are angled. Compared – *See this?* – a ripple of excitement undulating though the Maths room as every head switches round to check out *my* reaction as well as looking right to left. A few of the girls – Selina included – start casting me half-smiles, leaving me almost wishing I wasn't the only person I know without a mobile to take pictures of pizzas and zits and dogs turds with.

Having an iPhone would save me pinholing my eyes at Alistair Devlin's screen while the bell's ringing and there's a massive scramble to exit Stat's room.

Once Stat's scowled, 'I'm watching you, Mr Ryan,' to the empty seat beside me, only Nettie and I remain in the class.

'Is this true?' She waggles *her* mobile at me, her silvery eyes wide and shining. 'You're showcasing on nextbigthing? Wow!'

19
ZING GO THE STRINGS . . .

'What?'

'Nextbigthing.'

Nettie's voice is so whispery I've to move close to make her out. Interestingly, I discover doing this brings me out in goosepimples, and that she smells lemony. But I couldn't tell you what the Christmas she's on about, even after she repeats, carefully and considerably l-o-u-d-e-r, 'You're showcasing. On *nextbigthing*? My cousin's friend made an *amazing* viral too. Their album ***charted***. You're *so* lucky . . .' Nettie's nodding now. Enthusiastically. Her hair swishing. I get this urge to tangle my fingers through its thickness and hold it off her brow to see those silvery eyes better. And something else happens:

Ting!

This *sound* fills my skull. Kind of like an old-fashioned till ringing up a sale.

Ting!

There it goes again. A sound. Plus a sensation. And what a sensation! I'm not kidding; my skull reverberates as though it's trapped in a belfry during the Campanology World Championships.

Now, since I'm the picture of health, I can only assume this seismic activity is stemming from my heart. Possibly from the *strings* of my heart, like in that song Judy Garland sings: *Zing went the strings of my heart.*

Zinging. Halleluia. At last! Some of you are probably thinking right now: steamy hot teenage love action coming up pronto. But oh dear, I'm afraid steamy hot love action seekers are in for a disappointment.

Before I can stop myself, I'm barking at Nettie, 'What you on about?' in a rottweilery tone that has her cowing away from me.

'I'll download you. Forward you to everyone. See you,' she offers/threatens/promises. Scuttles off.

Oh! Give yourself a pat on the back there, Einstein. Ya muppet.

In my head Judy Garland's been replaced by Dad.

He sounds even more unimpressed with me than usual. For once I'm with him. There I was; enjoying the feeling of feeling comfortable with a girl who doesn't look like a hobbit, but who's really sweet and doesn't jellify me, like the mere thought of standing near only-in-your-dreams Selina does. We were just . . . just . . . just . . .

'Wait –'

I sprint off in pursuit of Nettie, but there's no sign.

Only this scrum of Sixth Years jostling into Media Studies. Seems the whole year's gathered. *Apart from her,* I realise, scanning the girls standing three and four to a chair.

I do, however, clock Selina. Then Lauren. Not before she sees me and swings up her arms so vigorously she loses her balance.

'Wah-hay, people. He's here.'

Despite having the combined weight of three girls plomping on her when she topples to the floor, Lauren continues to broadcast my entrance. She appears so excited at seeing me, I figure she's either taking the mick, or confusing me with someone else.

Elvis perhaps . . .

John Lennon . . .

The daft big lassie's actually *swooning* I realise, when Selina crouches down in her tight skirt. Whacks her pal a cracker on the cheek.

'Behave yourself, Lauren!' Selina snaps.

Then, before blood's had time to rush to Lauren's face and fingermark it, Selina's upright and – by the way this is **not** a dream sequence – she's slinking her spray-on shirt against me so her boobs rub my chest.

'Hi, Superstar,' she whispers in a voice that sounds like syrup dribbling over hot pancakes.

'That really *was* your CD on the bus, wasn't it?' Selina walks the tips of two fingers up my tie. Her face draws so close I count three blackheads on the end of her nose.

'Wh . . . what?' I flummox as something clasps my ankle, and a weight drags its way up my leg.

'I LOVE your video. And your *dancing* . . .' Lauren muscles between me and Selina, her full weight draping off my shoulders. For a moment I'm staring into Lauren's adoring eyes, open wide enough to swallow me. Then they come too close for me to focus and everything turns blank and something wet and warm and sluggy starts roving all over my lips . . .

'Snog!' a girl's voice shrieks, while I dart my eyes left and right of the squish that's rotating against my mouth. I see a cluster of faces. Male. Female. Cheering. Leering.

'My turn. Move!' a different girl's voice chimes. Could be Selina. Or Suzie. Who knows. I can't think straight. I mean girls who've *literally* never spoken to me are *literally* jabbing their tongues down my throat and licking the inside of my cheeks, their hands clutching mine. Planting them on waists, hips and . . . well. I won't spell it out . . .

'Jammy bastard.' Alistair Devlin whistles somewhere behind my head. If I could free my mouth from whoever's sucking lunch debris from the gaps between my teeth, I'd put him straight.

Mate, jammy nothing. It's surreal. I'm actually looking for Annette Moore? You seen her?

The most surreal thing of all is that Dad's song is blasting from speakers somewhere. And any Sixth Year not snogging me is singing along. Loud and raucous:

Storee of my

Storee of my

Storee of my life . . .

The drill of the interval bell finally ends my ordeal.

If I was capable of doing a head-count I'd reckon I've been smooched by every female in the room. Possibly even a couple of the guys.

'First useful lesson you've had in thirteen years, tiger.'

'Look a bit dazed there, Ro.'

Conspicuous by their absence while I was being molested, Barry and Smillie shoulder through the linger of girls who don't appear to have heard the bell.

'Time up,' Barry shoos them away.

'Hey, I'm Rory's mate. Still raring,' Smillie oscillates his tongue at the stragglers. That clears the room.

'D'you see what those girls *did* to me?' I mumble, my poor mouth feeling like it's been over-injected with dental anaesthetic.

'Did we *see*?' Smillie pulses his groin at me.

I concentrate on Barry.

'Why were they kissing me? And how come everyone knows Dad's song?'

Instead of giving me a straight answer, Barry flourishes his palms at the Media Studies computer.

'What? *What?*' I growl as Barry draws an air outline round me with both hands and moves over to the monitor like he's carrying a real picture. He places whatever he's virtually holding on the computer screen and stands back to admire it. The raised-eyebrow grin he gives me suggests I should be appreciating whatever he's 'hung' on the screen too. But I am NOT in the mood for crap mimes.

'I've Physics now. Talk!' I grab Barry's tie and strangle the knot.

'It's simple, Ro,' Barry croaks. '*Our* Bladester writes this monster song, right? *Right*?'

He waits for my reluctant shrug before continuing, 'Thing is – and no disrespect to Bladester, cuz he's awesome – but his image won't sell mainstream. And that's where *you* come in.'

'I *what*? Come in *where* . . .?'

Despite being jerked to his tiptoes by my chokehold, Barry beams into my scowling face, both hands drawing a fresh air outline round me.

'Thanks to us,' Barry proclaims, 'Fifteen Minute Bob is gonna be *massive*. In't he, Smiler?'

'Too right. A superstar.'

Before I can defend myself, Smillie has my cheeks in his hands and he's pulling me forward for *another* sodding kiss.

'Quit,' I fend him off, 'and tell me why you've put *me*

on a video, cuz I'm late for Physics.' *And lemony, silvery-eyed Annette's in Physics and I need to apologise to her for being a crabbit bugger.* I try to shoulder my way past Smillie but he catches my sleeve. Yanks me over to the computer.

'It's not a video you're on, brainbox. It's the WEB –'

'Worldwide, Ro. You're a viral –' Barry interrupts Smillie. His voice is ve-ry gentle, like he's preparing me for something. 'Better have a gander so you don't freak when babes hit on you again.'

'Wha?' I flap Barry's remark away, but he draws me to the computer.

'See. Thing is, if all goes to plan you're gonna be a download monster –'

'Like Gnarles Barkley. "*You make me CR-AZY* –"' Smillie cuts in and falsettos. Right in my ear.

'And the Arctic Monkeys,' Barry has to shout over the racket. 'Maybe Fifteen Minute Bob'll be even bigger. So check this, Ro.' Barry slings his arm round my shoulders. 'And don't have an epi, okay? We only uploaded you this morning –'

'Uploaded?'

I wriggle to free myself.

'Said DON'T have an epi. 'Member we're really doing

this for Bladester.' Barry tightens his grip. 'Look. Amazin'! Over seven hundred hits on *nextbigthing* already.'

I'm hearing those run-together words Annette used. They sound just as odd when Barry rushes them out, although now I understand what they mean.

'You've put *me* on a music download site?' I win a slow handclap for sounding the words I trace on the monitor.

'Don't tell us you've never heard of it!' Smillie sneers.

I don't.

'He's never heard of it.' Smillie ruffles my hair.

'Why put *me* there?'

'Cuz you're perfect, Ro,' Barry explains. 'See seven hundred and ninety-eight hits now. And risin', baby. All thanks to this.'

Barry's unfreezing the PAUSE on a mini-screen within the screen we're watching. 'PLAY 'Story of My Life' by Fifteen Minute Bob' an enthusiastic movie-trailer voice announces.

'You're rollin',' Barry says.

But I'm not. There's Dad. Pieces of him, anyway: His Nashville boots, his top hat, his silhouette, his voice, his harmonies, his Martin guitar, his lyrics, his sinewy dance moves . . .

From the moment his foot taps the opening bar of 'Story of My Life' to the final sepia fade, *everything* on screen is pure Dad.

Actually, backpedal that.

Apart from when all these stupid ugly stills of *me* flash up, the man I'm watching is Blade Ryan. Dad. But it's not Blade either. It's someone *more*.

Does that make sense?

I'm seeing a *version* of Dad. A version I've never met in the *flesh*. However, this Rock'n'Roll Blade-father is someone I've *imagined*.

See, because Dad's lived with the unfulfilled dream of becoming a bona fide song and dance man, *I've* lived with it too, visualising Dad being respected. Acclaimed . . .

I've even run dreams for him in my head:

Singing a knockout song to a sea of cheering fans in an enormodrome . . .

Picking up a Grammy, off of Prince or old Sir Cliff maybe . . .

Making a charity record with Elton and Eric and Annie . . .

I've imagined all this. Not because I've *wanted* to. Just because I've had to. So has Mum. Dad's promised us:

'*One day, yeah. Gonna be up there* –' So we've all lived Dad's dream. If you can call it living.

*But I **never** really believed . . . wow!*

During the 4.53 minutes I watch my mates' download, I forget the Physics I'm missing. Just lock on the screen, mesmerised by this new version of Dad. Oozing charisma. Radiating celebrity.

'But I wish I could see more of *Dad* singing. Have you mixed up two files? Cuz your promo's wonky. You've cut in all these stupid shots of *me*. Ruins the bits with Dad,' I tut during Barry's final frame. It's a neat ending too. Dad, filmed from behind, sweeps off his top hat, rests his guitar on his shoulder. Moseys into fadeout.

Down the Lost Highway . . .

The screen darkens from sepia to black, shrinks to a dot.

Mickey's drums thud. A solitary heartbeat.

'Epic innit?'

Smillie apes one of Dad's little dance shuffles. 'Home-made. Zero budget.' He points to a line of superscript text above Dad's video: **Stud Productions**.

'Yeah, but –' I try to be diplomatic. 'If you're filming *Dad*, why keep cutting to cruddy frames of me?'

'Huh?' Smillie scrunches up his face like I'm speaking Idiot.

I simplify. 'You never show Dad's face once.'

I click PLAY again.

My face blossoms from the tip of Dad's boot till eventually a huge close-up fills the screen. Then a slideshow runs until dozens of speccy mug-shots wall over the silhouette of Dad and his guitar.

'Folk'll think *I'm* Fifteen Minute Bob.' I gesture at the computer with the flat of my palm.

'Will they, by Jove!' Smillie holds my gaze, his eyes all twinkly with mischief. While he's doing this he delves into his jeans pockets. Roots about.

Deliberately, he cuts his gaze from me to the loose change in his hand, making a pantomime of choosing a penny. Breathing on it. Buffing it against his shirt before dropping the coin into my outstretched palm.

'Ro, you're my superbrain bro and beneath the snash I give out, I love you, man. You know that.' Barry cuffs me softly on the chin. 'But for a genius, you're well slow on the uptake sometimes.'

20

SCHOOL'S OUT

'You're *not* downloading me.'

'Shush it, will ya?'

Barry and Smillie are sneaking me between two bins outside the school kitchens. All very clandestine and unnecessary. But Barry's decided it's risky for me to stay on school premises: 'Cuz you're the next big thing on *nextbigthing*! That's why you *can't* pop into Doc Martin to ask for your Physics homework.'

'Forget that swotto shit anyway. Move on, Fifteen Minute Bob,' Smillie chips in. 'Female anatomy's the only science *you* need to know about now, FMB, and I'm here to learn you anything you wanna know in that department. *Any*thing.'

'Guys,' I change the subject. 'We're on camera. I'm a prefect, remember? Let's stay in school.'

Smillie boots me in the rump. '*"Hey, lithen guyths."* Christ, you sound like Sir bloody Cliff. How short *is* your memory? Remember those Sixth Year chicks? Want every dolly in school eating you alive? Cuz that's what's gonna happen now FMB's on phones and laptops and MP3s.'

'School's out!' Smillie, heedless of likely suspension, moons at the nearest CCTV.

'But I want to be an engineer, not a rock star,' I keep trying to reason with Barry. 'I've a Physics test tomorrow. And a debate about Jesus. Just take me off your film. Leave Dad singing. Actually, put more of him in. *I'll* do it for you –'

'Don't be a pie.' With a disbelieving chuckle, Barry elbows me into the nearest hedge. This is just as our bus arrives. Smillie has to yank me out someone's garden by the lapels of my blazer.

'Order! Order! School's out.' He swats the twigs out my hair. 'Whole world's watching you now.'

'But Dad's song's *nothing* to do with me. Why do I have to be on the video?' I insist while Barry and Smillie hussle me on the bus.

'We told you: You're the face of Fifteen Minute Bob. And his song *so* rocks everyone's gonna be wild for your geek-chic look. Ask Bladester about it,' Barry says, breenging to the back seat. 'His idea. He's your manager.'

'We're only groupie testers. And Security.' Smillie sniggers.

Security my arse. Barry and Smillie don't even *pretend* to keep up when I jump the bus early. Sprint home.

'Oi!' Bursting into the flat I launch myself at Dad, whirling him round to face me before I realise he's on the phone.

'No *way* am I being you.' I grip Dad's forearm. He stares at my hand then pulls a mocking face.

'Sorry, excuse me a sec–' he says into the receiver. His voice is bright and clipped. His drawl vanished. 'Disturbance outside.'

Dad's phoney-phone tone fades as he clamps the mouthpiece.

'Dealing with a record company here, for fuck's sake.' His flinty glare withers my grip.

'S–Sorry,' I hear myself bleat like I'm six and Dad's a proper dad. One who gets snarked when sons interrupt while he's doing business. Dad's apologising too. That new voice again. 'Sorry. As I say, any legal offer comes to Simon Anthony Management. Oh, excuse me again, please –'

Although I splurt, 'Simon Anthony, is it?' when I hear Dad referring to himself by his real name, *I'm* not the cause of this second interruption. It's Bob Blade this time, his chorus to 'Downbeat Lover-Man' jangling from the back pocket of Dad's leather jeans.

'Need to take another call,' Dad gabbles to the first caller whose voice – American, male – yatters from the receiver Dad's dumped on the hall table. This is so he has both hands free to prod at his mobile. 'Aw, man. How do these crazy things . . .?'

'Green button,' I sing-song. Smug. I use Dad's fumbling Luddite panic as my excuse to glare suspiciously at the mobile – *How come it's receiving calls? Who set that ringtone? Where'd the cash come for a SIM card?*

'Hi. Simon Anthony Management. Can you hold?'

As Dad recovers his composure, he turns away from me again. Juggles two conversations at once:

'This is Mr Anthony. And you are . . .?'

'*Sorry* about that, Stewart. Where were we . . .?'

'Haven't you, Roger? Well I've heard of *you* . . .'

'Oh we're *incredibly* excited about Fifteen Minute Bob too. I'm delighted you're interested all the way from the U S of A . . .'

'Just Fifteen Minute Bob. We like the enigma factor, Stewart: *Who is he? Where'd he come from*? Good for buzz. Music industry loves a mystery: Lady Ga Ga. Seasick Steve. Badly Drawn Boy. Sting . . . well maybe not Sting . . .'

'Roger, I'm new to management, but been in this business . . . oooh thirty years . . .'

'Yes. FMB *does* sound mature for a youngster . . . Careworn voice and a cute face . . . You like the image? So do we. And oh, yes, *can* he dance . . . What's that? The *best* new voice this year? I'll pass on the compliment, but let me tell you, Stewart, he's the sweetest, humblest . . .'

'*My* background, Roger? Well, basically more creative than management.'

'No, sorry; no email yet. We've been snowed under, Stewart. Everyone wanting their piece of FMB.'

'More songs? Sheesh. The boy's written albumsful . . . Putting out a slow ballad online next . . .'

'One-hit wonder? You for real, Stewart? You've only heard the tip of the iceberg, if that makes sense. Ha ha ha . . .'

'No, best I scoot over to you, Roger. We're remodelling . . . Never too busy for lunch, though.'

'Tell the truth, you're not the first tiger to bite, Stewart. But by all means, talk numbers . . .'

'I know that hotel. Classy. Didn't *Bob Blade* stay there last time he hit town . . .?'

'*Love* to do business, Stewart. You have a nice day yourself.'

21

WORLD GONE WRONG

'Man, these suits are freakin' my noodle.'

I watch Dad attempting to roll a fag, but his fingers are so trembly, tobacco dandruffs his Grateful Dead T-shirt. When the phone suddenly rings again, he twitches with such a spasm, the cigarette paper he's holding flutters from his grip.

'All day, man.' Dad clamps his hands to his ears, his knees buckling so he sinks to the floor. Soon as his backside touches the carpet, the mobile jingle-jangles in a key that jars horribly with the ringing house-phone. To add to this cacophony, the letterbox flap-snaps like a nervous starting pistol.

'Blaaaaa-dester!' Smillie's voice hollers outside the flat.

'Where's our razor-sharp supa-star hiding?' Barry's foot wellies his corny pun home. Unamused, I thumb my mates inside.

By this time Dad's spreadeagled on the hall floor, moaning to himself.

'Wassup, Bladester? Bin at de jungle juice?'

Smillie, *totally* misreading the situation, flops on to the carpet. Tokes on something invisible.

Barry has more insight. He hunkers over Dad.

'Kicked off madstyle?'

Retrieving Dad's mobile, Barry switches it off. A moment of silence settles. *Letting in a precious chink of something lost,* I realise. Just as the house-phone shrills again.

'D'you know Bob Blade said somewhere once you put your face on the dollar, everybody can spend you till you're done?' Dad groans, rolling his head from side to side. 'And Bob was right. Record companies. Press. *nextbigthing* suits callin', callin', callin'. After their little dimes of FMB. Griping how my phone's busy.' Dad flaps a weary hand at me, 'Which is why, before *you* start a-carpin', Einstein – I used my precious Ria's credit card to buy call-time on *this* –'

From the ground, Dad taps my shin with his mobile. 'And hey – don't bother reminding me what your mum's gonna say 'bout spendin' her bread. I know I'm a dead man walkin'.'

'Nah, Mrs Bladester'll be cool when she finds about about all *this.*' Ever the optimist, Barry brandishes Dad's mobile aloft. Like it's a Grammy. A Brit. An Ivor Novello.

Instead of mirroring Barry's grin, Dad shrugs.

'Thirty years trying 'n' suddenly . . . *maaan*. Sure don't feel like I thought I'd feel when I got what I wanted. Did Bob say that? Or did I? *Maaan.*'

Dad clamps his hands to his face. 'Feels like my world's fallin' away from under my feet. I'm danglin' in mid-air,' he sighs through his fingers. Then under his breath, he starts singing:

'D'you know what it's like,'

'To lose the ground

Cuz I've just be found

Though I've been a-round . . .'

And over the words Dad lullabies to himself, our phone shrills and drills. No one answers it.

Well, *I* daren't. What if some big-shot's on the line?

And Mum's not home to answer the phone.

'Hey, by the way, didn't Mum's shift finish hours ago?' I turn to quiz Dad.

But the slippery old goat's not here either. Must have escaped under camouflage of his own masterpiece. It's blaring from the computer, *nearly* loud enough to drown the bloody dring-dring, dring-dring, dring-dring . . .

'Jeez, Bladester. You're right about the emails pouring in.'

'Check the feedback: five stars everywhere –'

'Loads here comparing you to the real Bob Blade himself –' Barry and Smillie yell in relay.

Pointlessly.

Because the real Fifteen Minute Bob has left the building.

22

LOTTO BALLS IN MY HEAD

'Forgot your bloody key?' I'm sarking at this blur shifting outside the front door, assuming Dad's back already.

But I'm wrong.

Worse than that, I'm offering the *rudest* of welcomes to the first and only girl to pay me a housecall.

Bollocks.

Just get this *feeling* that I've dingied Nettie. Not in my head. Lower down. Chest area. There'll likely be a rational explanation for this sensory recognition of an unseen subject: Perhaps my peripheral vision captured a subconscious glimpse of her outline, and it sneaked along my optic nerve. Or maybe a rising air current wafted microscopic particles of her lemony scent up my nostrils, thus triggering olefactory memory and . . .

Anyway, science-schmience.

The longer I ponder, the further Nettie's retreating from my life.

'WAIT!' I bellow over her dying footfall, loud enough for Moran the Moron to hear over the chinkle of a one-arm bandit paying out in his casino across town, never mind from his flat upstairs.

In the gloom of the bottom landing, I catch Nettie's arm.

'Sorry. Thought you were my dad. He's done a runner,' I pant, wishing, as she turns to face me, and I touch her for the first time, that it wasn't Dad's ropy old arm I was being reminded of at this particular moment. How tough its sinews felt beneath their leathery hide when I grabbed *him* earlier. Like tattooed beef jerky, compared to Nettie. Her forearm is velvet soft, ever so plump where it swells to meet her elbow. Although everything else about Nettie is slight. Her wrist so tiny I could encircle it twice with my fingers. She is *far* too delicate to look after herself.

That's one of the reasons I don't want to let her go.

The other is that I have *so* much to say to her:

Hey, didn't mean to bite your head off when you kept saying nextbigthing earlier.

Just didn't understand.

But I do now.

That's why I was angry when you rang the bell.

Wasn't mad with you, Nettie – zit okay to call you that, by the way?

Seems to kinda suit you.

You're so pretty.

Any chance I'll ever kiss you?

Got the most amazing hair – thick and black like treacle. But not sticky.

And I love how you smell.

Lemony. Kinda like Lidl's washing-up liquid.

'Please don't go.'

My head's gone haywire, all my thoughts and words suddenly churning, tumbling, rotating. Just like those crazy ping-pong balls.

You know?

From the Lotto?

'Come back upstairs.' That's one of the things I *do* say. Because Nettie shrugs.

'Okay,' she says. And that's when a pair of familiar voices from the landing above snort,

'Yeah! Come on up, baby.'

'Let's experiment on each other!'

'Rory, we're being filmed,' Nettie gasps.

Of course Barry and Smillie are safe behind my front door with the camera before I can say, 'You're dead meat.'

'Ooopsies,' chimes Barry through the letterbox. 'Rory's on the warpath. So loved up he didn't see us filming.'

'Wanna see your coupon,' Smillie brays. '"*You're dead meat.*" Pure psycho, man.'

'Let me in, please.' I struggle to keep my dignity and temper, no easy feat when Barry and Smillie are lying on my hall floor with their legs in the air like shameless dogs waiting to be tickled. Pair of them are holding the camera between them.

'Oh man, check Rory's goo-eyes.'

'*Ah luv yoo, Nettie. But I'd love you more with your top off . . .*'

For a guy who's barely scraped an English exam, Smillie's impressively creative when it comes to producing instant dialogue for Barry's video, complete with a Scandanavian porn-star identity for poor Nettie.

By the way, I am *not* reproducing *any* of Smillie's lines. It's mortifying enough to hear what my landfill-brain mate spouts while the Muse behind his mind-muck is squinched up next to me, her breath tickling my ear. I'm not proud to admit the nearness of Nettie triggers a little private movie of my own. Told you I'm not perfect, didn't I?

Mind you, no wonder I'm in a lather. We're *so* close our faces meld as we peer through the letterbox to watch our innocent exchange sullied by Barry's jumpy camera-work. Nettie's cheek is soft and cool. Mine a roaring Bunsen burner. I wouldn't blame her shifting away. Leaving me here. Never speaking to me again.

However she does neither. In fact she kind of takes control.

'No point you reasoning with that pair. I'll handle this.' She squeezes my shoulder, her gesture more calming than flirtatious. But I'm hardly complaining.

'Hey, Oli-ver,' Nettie sing-songs. She's just audible over Smillie experiencing what I assume is a fake, movie-style orgasm.

'Shut up, Oliver,' Nettie persists.

Smillie quits panting to bat his eyelashes into the letterbox. 'Don't see how you're gonna make me. And don't call me Oliver.'

'Made you already, Oliver,' Nettie bites back, 'but smut

on and everyone'll hear about Greece last summer. Oliver tell you 'bout that, Barry?'

Nettie raises her voice enough to stop Barry fiddling with the camcorder.

'Yeah. I met Oliver in Corfu. Was with my cousin. We're same height, same build. Same hair,' Nettie continues, although Smillie appears stricken with a hacking cough.

'My cousin's a guy, though. Oliver couldn't tell.' Nettie's digging my ribs. 'Followed us like a little lost puppy. Don't worry, I've kept the note you wrote our Brian. Might show some of the girls, Oliver . . .' Nettie's voice drops half an octave. ''Less you let us in and scrub that film right now, okay?'

To my delight Smillie's scrabbling with the door-chain before Nettie's finished delivering her ultimatum. 'We'll do what she says, Baz. Can film you 'n' Lauren instead. Be sexier than Rory anyway –'

'No chance.'

Through the letterbox I watch Barry shooing Smillie into the sitting room. 'So what if you tried to pull a bloke? When you're desperate you're desperate.' Barry ends the matter by turning his attention to me. 'Sorry. We gotta edit ‘n’ upload some fresh FMB footage asap to keep things hot online. So give us fifteen minutes, Ro. Geddit? Make yourselves comfy out there.’

From the wink Barry cocks me before he drops the letterbox, you’d think he was doing me a favour. Leaving me out on the stairwell with Nettie Muir.

23
LOVE IS BLINDING

An hour later, me and Nettie are still taking turns at the letterbox.

'Barry's answering my phone. Cheek!'

'Ugh. Smillie's taking a leak with the bog door open.'

'Oi. Wash your *hands*. And don't go into my room –'

'Oliver, don't go in Rory's room.'

I can't speak for Nettie, but I'm climbing the walls. If doormat bristles digging into my knees wasn't hellish enough, hearing my phone pretty much ring off the hook is diabolical. Barry only answers it once. Keeps cutting his eyes to the letterbox while he's talking to the caller. Looks sheepish as he puts the receiver down. Like someone's given him an ear-bashing. Mum, I'm wild-guessing.

Over the brain-drilling phone, Nettie suggests at one point we annoy Barry and Smillie by ringing the bell non-stop. 'When they belt out to make us quit,' she rehearses a head-butt, 'we *ram* the puddings.

Nick the camera. Lock *them* –'

Can't. Our neighbours complain enough about the stramash Dad makes, coming home drunk and stuff, I want to tell Nettie, but she might do one if she discovers our flat's on an Environmental Health final warning for noise pollution.

'Let's just sit and wait.' I slump on the nearest stair. Sigh to my soles.

'Oh, Rory!' Nettie drops down beside me. 'You're welcome at mine, 'cept my dad doesn't know I've sneaked out. I'm meant to be studying so he'll freak if I turn up with some hot guy out the blue. He'll phone my mum. Start giving out about me turning into a tarty slapper too, or something. Sorry.' Nettie bumps her arm against mine, the gesture comforting and flirty at the same time. The all-over blush it activates pipes heat through my veins like a central heating system firing up.

'But your mates can't be doing this to you. Phone them,' she urges.

'No mobile.' I shrug.

'You really need looking after, mister,' Nettie whispers. I tell you, her words warm me like a blast from a blowtorch.

'Use this.' She pushes her own phone into my hand.

So I call Barry. Hear the faint organ whirl of Bob Blade's 'Lone Trails and Neverendin' Highways' start up through the landing wall I'm leaning against before cutting off.

'Voicemail.' I shrug again. 'Waste of time calling Smillie, either.'

'Hey. Who else is on your side? Apart from me.'

Nettie half-pats, half-squeezes my hand.

'Could try my mum's work.'

Nettie watches over me while I dial. Elbows propped on her knees, hands cupping her chin, I wonder if she has the slightest idea how cute she looks, her eyes glittery pewter in the dark, or realises what the little frown quirking her brow is doing to my heart. I'm surprised she doesn't hear the tattoo it's drumming inside my chest. Out here on the landing it sounds as loud to me as the persistent shrill of the phone.

'Not your night, is it, Rory?'

Across the top of Nettie's mobile, our eyes meet. Lock. The hall phone keeps ringing. A faint scrape and skuffle rises from the landing below. A door creaks. Inner or outer I can't tell, although a sudden draught swirls around us. Despite these disturbances, a stillness shrouds Nettie and me. And I know this is scientifically impossible, but the moment feels like it's ours. We're the only people in the world and it's stopped turning. Just so time can stand still and we can sit, on a cold stair, looking into each other's eyes.

'Thanks anyway,' I whisper, goosebumps swelling from the root of every follicle on my body.

'For what? We're friends.' Nettie's eyes hold mine. And before my inner debater stymies the first test of my life that doesn't involve decimal points or test-tubes –

Do it.

***Don't** do it. She'll pull away.*

***DO** it! –*

I'm holding Nettie's hand and the rest of her is moving closer, just like bodies do in the movies, until her front is pressed against me and her features blur out of focus (not just because my specs are carefully removed) and my lips are brushed by something soft and warm, and my nostrils zing with lemon zest and my ears pop gently as if there are mini-fireworks celebrating Rory's First Proper Kiss . . .

OK, OK: I know this might be t.m.i if you hate the nitty-gritty of other folk getting it on, but I can't help analysing this sensory rush overwhelming me.

The result of one pair of lips touching another.

Extraordinary!

I'm even experiencing the sensation of *lights* flashing in my peripheral vision. Orange and strong. Their brightness so scorching I swear their heat energy penetrates my closed eyelids. Wow!

Even when Nettie ends our first kiss and draws away with a gasp, the lights continue to dazzle. Still popping around my head. To the sound of muffled thuds. Exactly like mini-fireworks in the distance of a November night . . .

Or flashbulbs going off in my face . . .

Duh!

Of course I'm only being photographed, amn't I? Face on. Close-up. Dazzled by lights, I can't even *see* Nettie while I grope about to find where she laid my specs. I only hear her voice on the landing below – 'Hey. What you taking pictures for?'

Suffice to say, the world's turning again. Spinning, more like. I'm blundering about with my arms in front of me. Flashbulb ghosts still blinding me.

I don't find my specs till I scrunch them underfoot.

'Nettie? Annette?' I bleat, making for this jumble of voices I can hear on the bottom landing. I only realise how close I am to the shape in front of me when my outstretched fingers jab something bristly and wet.

'Oi, mind my gasper and stop pawing me, Einstein. You can't have missed me much with sweet little cherry-lips keeping you company.'

Against the surface of my palm, Dad's lips move like some gellid sea-creature. The shock of actually touching him restores my vision, although with no specs, the world's a blur. I only vaguely recognise this second bloke who's hovering behind Dad. His grin exposes too many teeth when Dad cocks his head at me.

'There's your hot ticket himself. Caught in action with one of his fans.'

'Smashing!'

This second bloke's catchphrase rings a bell. But I only place him as the reporter from our local paper (who interviewed me about my winning seagull photo – 'Smashing!') after I'm outside, peering through peening rain at Nettie. She's busy tussling with a different man who's twice her height and girth, trying to wrestle a camera out his hands. Before I have any opportunity to play the gallant, Nettie's camera-man lofts it out of her reach – hardly a challenge when she's the size of nonsense. Then he legs it into a passing cab.

'Someone musta phoned those creeps to sniff about cuz of your download.' Nettie glowers, covering her face too late for camera-man to pap us both from the cab.

'What you fighting that gorilla for?' I reach out to touch Nettie's arm, but she's too stoked to let me near.

'He's invading your privacy.' She stabs at the disappearing cab. 'OK, you've a song out. Doesn't make you public property. Let's boot out those other slimeballs now –'

'Tricky that.' Putting my hands on Nettie's shoulders before she plunges back into battle, I take a deep breath.

'One of those guys is my dad. This *nextbigthing* business is his doing,' I wince. Cringe. However, to my surprise Nettie's shoulders relax.

'The crazy hair one? Leather coat to his ankles? Eyeliner?'

I'm nodding gravely, till I realise Nettie's giggling.

'Rory, you are SO alike . . .' Nettie giggles again. 'Though he's a bit more . . . well . . . bit more rock'n'roll.'

'A bit,' I sigh. *Messed up. Wasted. Useless.* Bitter adjectives rise up in my throat. I swallow them down with the words. 'And we're *not* alike actually.'

Nettie narrows her eyes. 'I'm sorry. You *are*.'

When I don't respond she grins. 'Christ, my poor dad's a fart in a cardigan. That's why my mum ran off with one of her students. Imagine having an old man who looks like Alice Cooper and gets away with it. Sweet.' Nettie keeps trying to nudge me. Lighten me up.

'You think *that* makes a good dad?' I bridle. 'Dad might look like a fun guy, but there's no fun living with him. He's a loser. And I can't talk to him about anything either. He's useless,' I'm splurting before I can stop myself.

'Oooh.' Nettie steps back. 'That was harsh. Your dad can't be a total screw-up. Look how you've turned out.'

All Mum's doing. She's the only reason I'm not fucked up, I nearly splutter. But there's so much more I'd need to go into after that. *All of it too much too soon and too depressing for me and Nettie right now,* I decide. I just circle my arm in the air.

'Look. Bottom line? My dad's not half as much fun as he looks. He just suits himself. This Fifteen Minute Bob mess? His fault. Including us being stuck out on the landing all night –'

'Oh, that was just a mess was it?'

'No. I didn't mean –'

Before I dig my pit any deeper and Nettie walks away leaving me at the bottom of it, I grab her hand. 'Listen, I just mean I shouldn't be on *nextbigthing*,' I babble. 'It's Dad's bright idea. So is Barry and Smillie filming. Dad's stolen my identity to have a hit. And, by the way, that's *Dad's* song on that website. He's Fifteen Minute Bob. It's not me –'

'Hey, hey. Slow down.' Nettie silences me by pressing her finger to my lips. She shows me her wristwatch. 'Listen, it's so late I'm dead if I don't head. So,' she goes up on tiptoes to whisper, 'why don't you go home too. Try having a chat with your dad. Find out what he's up to. I'll phone later.'

'Can't you just come up? Dry off? I'll walk you home, after –'

'After?' Nettie's eyebrows arch. '*After?* And you *don't* take after your wild old man?' she gasps as if I've suggested something inappropriate. Steps back.

'Oh, I didn't mean . . . it's just . . . you're soaked and . . .'

'*Kidding!* Lighten up.' Nettie squeezes my hands

till I stop stammering. 'I'd love to come up, but I can't, so here's the deal –' kissing my cheek, she lets me go, fluttering her fingers in goodbye. 'If you talk to your dad, I promise I'll come up next time. When it's just us two.'

24
MUM'S MELTDOWN

Although I'm in a puddle up to my ankles, the exquisite prospect of having a . . . a . . . a . . . *girl – me!* – heats the space between my ribs as if there's a mug of something toasty pressed to my chest. I only realise my shirt is glued to me like a sub-zero second skin when a hand smoothes the fabric against my back. Brrr!

'Science research on hypothermia is it, pet?'

Mum dunts me back to reality with the shopper she swings into the crook of my knees. 'If not, you're dafter than your father,' she mutters.

Oh dear.

'Where've you been, Mum?'

Sensing trouble, I make my accusation chirp like chat, nodding Mum ahead of me as I take her shopping from her.

'Nail bar. Massage. Hairdresser. Cocktails. The usual.'

I decide against pressing Mum for the truth. Just

keep schtoom till she lets herself into the flat, then dodge past her. Wise decision.

'Si-mon?'

Mum's shrill strafes like automatic rifle-fire. It sends Barry and Smillie scurrying from the dining room as if someone's just plugged in one of those sonar devices that rids your house of pests.

'Hi, Mrs Ryan.'

'Bye, Mrs Ryan.'

'See ya, Ro.'

Rats abandoning a sinking ship. Lucky them. From the kitchen I watch Mum strip off her coat and cast it to the floor like a matador.

'Simon, why's there *nothing* in our bank account?' She storms into the sitting room. 'I'd to leave half the shopping at the checkout, and borrow twenty quid from a junior nurse. How d'you think that feels, Simon? You promised to find work. But I'm home off a double shift and you're eating fecking takeaway with some new pal you've picked up –'

Although I make as much noise as I can while I'm unpacking, I hear Mum loud and clear. Putting stuff away doesn't take long anyway: A loaf of marked-down bread.

Split wrapper. Couple of tins minus labels – could be dog food. Wouldn't be the first time. Germoline-coloured saver brand ham. No fruit. No veg.

I open a box of cheapo cornflakes. They pour like sawdust, grey and dusty. It's a relief to find there's no milk. *Not hungry, really*. Scooping Mum's coat from where she flung it, I pause outside the sitting room. Gone quiet in there.

My hand hovers on the door handle. But I don't enter the room. I'm remembering how fiercely Mum hates me caught in domestic crossfire.

She'd rather I was tackling my homework I decide, peeling a couple of twenty-quid notes from the telescope fund I hide between the Dad-proof pages of my science dictionary. In the hall I unzip Mum's handbag. Delve for her purse.

But the inside of the bag's a blurry Tardis. I'm so busy squinting into it, shifting bills and headache pills and letters and lipsticks without rustling or jangling or clicking anything too loudly, I don't realise the reporter bloke's at my shoulder, tapping his biro against his dirty yellow teeth.

''Ello. 'Ello. 'Ello, *nextbigthing* with his fingers in the pie. Smashing! Remember me?' The reporter's staring pointedly at the money I'm still holding.

'Angus Graham. Firing copy into the Red Tops this weather. Anything celeb. Anything juicy. Smashing!' The reporter nods approvingly at his own career summary, then lowers his voice. 'Listen, Captain Solly Beaumont in there's saying no interviews –'

'– Captain Solly who?' I interrupt.

'Y'know; was Bob Blade's manager way back in the mists.' Angus Graham snorts, cocking his head at the sitting room. His eyes stay glued to Mum's handbag. 'But while he's tied up with the old trouble and strife, howz about you tell me what it feels like to hit the charts running with your very first download?' The reporter talks at my hands while I'm stuffing notes into Mum's purse. 'Cooperate, 'n I'll write you up nice. Don't wanna kick off your career with bad press, believe me –'

'Career?'

Could my life turn more surreal?

'I'm a Sixth Year with Physics homework for tomorrow. That's your story.' I make a deliberate show of pulling shut the zip on Mum's bag: No Comment.

Unfortunately my metaphorical mime ballses up,

because Mum's zip snags. I have to reopen the handbag. Free a leaflet caught in the metal teeth.

I smooth it out to make sure it's not torn.

But when I see what it is . . . Christ. Wish I'd shredded it to scraps.

It's a job application. Completed. Dated tomorrow. For a Senior Nurse Manager position.

In Vancouver, I gulp.

The neatness of Mum's printing flips my stomach. Every capital letter is uniform in size. Nothing scored out. Nothing dashed off in haste:

Name. Date of Birth. Nationality.

No!

I'm reading what Mum's put for Marital Status: **SEPARATED**.

Although the word's only been written in pencil, and faintly, each character Mum's fitted into a box blooms and shimmers in front of my eyes. When her voice drifts from the sitting room, she sounds likes she's an ocean away already.

'. . . And none of these VISA transactions are mine: Recording studio. Liquor Shack. A mobile phone contract. That went through *today*.'

'Smashing!'

I've forgotten the reporter's still here till he kisses his fingers at me, head cocked towards Mum's voice.

'One song out and you're Amy Winehouse. Love it!' He taps my shoulder with his notebook. 'How's this? "Too much. Too fast. Too young."' He blocks imaginary copy in the air. '*Talent oozes from his pores,*' he scribbles as he talks, '*but download sensation Fifteen Minute Bob robs Matron Mum to feed drugs and booze habit* . . . Listen,' the reporter shrugs, 'that's printed. 'Less you gimme something from the horse's mouth –'

When all I give is a snort, the reporter clicks the top of his pen. Opens the front door.

'Smashing!'

But before he takes his lies anywhere, I snatch his notebook out his hand. 'Some reporter, missing the scoop right under your nose,' I tell Angus Graham as I'm crossing the hall into the bathroom. Over the toilet I start ripping pages from the reporter's notebook. Dumping his crap lies where they belong.

'Oi, take my advice. Stunts like this won't buy you fame, sonny,' Angus Graham yells over the gushing cistern. Before his swirling scraps disappear, he plunges his arm into the water.

'Take *my* advice: better dry-clean the jacket. Last person didn't flush.' I wink at the reporter's soaked sleeve. I don't hang about to show him out.

'Rory, where d'you get *that*?' Mum gasps when she sees the application form I'm brandishing.

'Fell out your handbag,' I white-lie. 'What's it about?' I glance from Mum to Dad. Double take. He's slumped on the settee, togged up in a smart-casual jumper. *Chinos*. Sorta weekend sports-casual attire Smillie's old man goes in for. Dad looks all wrong. It's like seeing Iggy Pop dressed like Prince Philip.

'Whassis?'

'Thought I'd better sharpen up to meet the suits. Simon Anthony Management look –' Dad frowns down at himself like his torso belongs to somebody else.

'It's three hundred pounds of nonsense on Visa, Simon. And it's what's driven me to *this*.'

Mum snatches the job application from my hand. 'And I'm sorry, Rory. This is a great job I'm applying for. Going to make us way more comfortable money-wise if I go for it. But nothing's decided yet, I promise,' she tells me softly without taking her eyes from Dad. 'And you weren't meant to find out this way, I promise that too. But the thing is,' she sighs, touching my cheek lightly, 'you'll be leaving school, sweetheart. Away to university. I have to make plans for me. Don't want to keep living like this.'

As she leaves the sitting room, Mum adds, 'I'm giving your dad one last chance to decide if he still wants to stay part of this family while I'm on night-shift –'

'You're working *again*? Mum, you've not eaten or –'

'Sweetheart, we're skint.' From the hall, Mum's voice is matter of fact.

'I've given you money. I can give you more. Hang on.' I'm behind Mum, towering over her, my arm itching to grab her.

'Rory.' Without turning, Mum finds my hand. Squeezes. 'Your child should *never* have to do that,' she speaks more than loud enough for Dad to hear.

'Ria.'

Dad, in his sensible new clothes, is framed in the sitting room doorway.

'Don't go, Ria,' he says. 'Please. I'll change. Get a new job.'

Normally Mum snorts whenever Dad promises that.

But tonight she scoops up her handbag like nobody spoke.

'Man, she's *serious*.'

When Dad gestures at Mum's receding footsteps, he looks so shell-shocked, I almost feel sorry for him.

Almost.

But then I remember all the bad stuff. It rises from my guts; muck oozing a backed-up drain.

'Course Mum's serious. You've wrecked her life. Wasted yours. Stolen mine,' I scowl.

Two hours later, I still haven't answered a single Physics question.

25

NORTH STAR

Why am I so upset? It's not like I'm a stranger to Mum and Dad's meltdowns. Tonight's didn't even come close to being the most searing ding-dong they've had – albeit it was the most 'ultimate': I mean, Mum's always threatening to cross the Irish Sea back to Kerry, but the Atlantic?

I suppose the prospect of that is the reason why I just can't knuckle down to that Physics worksheet Nettie delivered.

Not because I don't *understand* the questions – they're doddly. I just don't understand the point of doing them. Not tonight. When Nettie might be my girlfriend. Mum might be separating from Dad. Going to Vancouver. A crock of shit might be all over the papers tomorrow. And I'm supposed to be Fifteen Minute Bob.

Plus it's really tricky to concentrate with Dad singing. He's at the kitchen table.

Door open. And although he began crooning softly,

he's rapidly cranked his volume. I don't mean Dad's doing a Rage Against the Machine, I just mean he's putting welly into his voice. It's like he's performing. Trying to nail a take. This is what lures me away from Physics to investigate.

Passing the hall table I notice Barry's camcorder. Don't ask me why, but I flick it to **RECORD**.

Dad doesn't notice me creeping up. He's strumming too hard. Puffing his mouth organ like it's a peak-flow meter. He's unaware I'm behind him, training my lens where he's sprawled between two chairs. Changed back into more typical Dad leisure gear – leather trousers, clogs, and a black string vest – *zoom* – his spindly legs are twisted like liquorice laces on one kitchen chair, splayed-out torso on the other. Head thrown back, he doesn't open his eyes. Just his mouth.

'So this is how love feels
When you've found your true North Star,
And all those days wanderin'
Still lead back to where you are,'

Dad sings, and his voice . . . well . . . how can I put this? All the sweetness that makes him a completely different singer from Bob Blade is there, but there's also a rawness I've never heard before. Dad sounds . . . I don't know . . . like his ribcage is cranked open so his heart's exposed and the pain of *that* is what I'm hearing.

Sorry. What a pathetic, touchy-feely analysis. Subjective too. But I lack the musical vocabulary to define what's happening with Dad. All I know is that something intense is taking place in my kitchen, and even though Dad is probably singing about personal stuff he's never said to Mum, and never will, something about his song touches me. Transports me back in time to those moments earlier tonight when I sat on that cold stair *aching* to kiss Nettie . . .

Nettie . . .

I'm trying to keep Barry's camera steady while Dad yowls:

'And it's true to say

I should never have roamed

Baby, though I've lost my way

Your light beckons me home. Bollocks. Not good enough.'

– and his singing actually re-conjures the lower-limb swoopy melt I experienced when Nettie's lips found mine. Honestly, I nearly drop the bloody camcorder.

Lucky I don't, because Dad's righting his chair to rewrite something scrawled on the ripped-off top of the sawdust cornflakes packet. While he refreshes himself with a long pull from the whisky bottle at his elbow, I retreat. Instinct's advising me not to disturb him, you see. He seems to be finding it tricky enough to work lyrics round the melody his fingers keep repeating on guitar.

'*You're my diamond in the darkest night . . . diamond in the da . . .*' Dad twists the note he's singing to a groan. 'Piss poor.' He tries again: '*Gonna tell the world. Aw* – Ria!' producing another painful groan. And suddenly the waver and break in his voice reminds me of yet another song by guess who.

Now I'm not going into the nitty-gritty of why Dad picked this particular Bob Blade number called 'Confessin' My Regrets' to play on non-stop rotation for a month about two years ago. All you need to know is there was a fling. Young. Dutch, she was. Dad was very, very sorry when Mum caught him. As for the song, it's one Bob Blade wrote during his 'Finding God' period in the early 1990s. So it's an expression of devotion, and Blade is so focussed on conveying how he feels about his Maker that his vocal is all over the place. Cracked. Out of tune.

Punctuated by the moans that come out when you're draped over a toilet with food poisoning. Hey, but he gets his message across. And that's the thing about certain songs, I suppose. Perfect delivery can be incidental to sincerity, whether it's Bob Blade himself testifying to the Lord, or my dad, knotted up over his guitar, admitting:

'You're a guiding light in my dark night

Of the soul –'

Considering how the phone rang off the hook earlier, it's spookily karmic how I have peace to train the camcorder on Dad for so long without interruption.

Especially when a cunning plan is hatching in my head.

This is too good to be true, I keep thinking while I zoom in on Dad's face and his fretwork, panning the length of his guitar. Because Dad's lost in his music, he doesn't move much, so I don't need to jerk the lens about to follow him. I just try to keep a steady hand. Over an hour of footage I steal. It includes Dad singing his complete chorus for the first time:

Now I'm such a fool to lose you,

When your hand reached out to lead me,

Your light shone but I closed my eyes,

Now you say that you don't need me,

Please don't leave.

I can't live when you're far,

You'll always be my North Star.

Once Dad has sung these lines for the third or fourth time, he makes a tipsy attempt to rise, but his legs don't play ball. With a drunken sigh he plumps up the sawdust cornflakes box and pillows his head on it. Two seconds later, he's snoring. Nearly as loud as the phone. It starts ringing while I'm gathering all Dad's scribbled lyrics together. I don't take the call till I've covered Dad's shoulders with a quilt. Turned out the kitchen light. Closed the door while I'm tiptoeing out.

That American record bloke Dad talked to earlier – Stewart – calls me Simon.

I don't correct him.

Just remind him it's the middle of the night over here.

'Hey, appreciate. But business is business,' Stewart hollers. I picture him pacing shale on the edge of the Atlantic ocean, shouting into a can with a hole pierced in the bottom. String connecting him to me.

'Just need to hear another song so we know FMB's career gonna have legs. Then a contract's on the table.'

While Stewart's voice is crackling down the line, I eject the video disc from Barry's camcorder. Test its weight in my palm:

Nothing.

Everything.

'New song coming up, Stewart,' I promise. 'Plus video.'

26

THE NEW FIFTEEN MINUTE BOB

Move over Spielberg and Lucas. There's a new kid in town!

By the time my alarm trills me up for school at 6.52 a.m., I've produced a complete video for 'North Star'. All without a crew or a Winnebago or an entourage. All performed by the *new* Fifteen Minute Bob.

I've kept things simple: plenty footage of Dad's fingerwork and as little as possible of his hard-knock-life face. Any close-ups are doctored by a battery of useful effects I found up the computer's sleeve: Vaselining, shadowing, fading. I don't muck about with my film to be smart-arsy. Just to minimise trauma should some unfortunate kiddo google 'North Star', expecting some astronomy link. Only to stumble on to *nextbigthing* and a slack-jawed, rheumy-eyed soak, yowling like his heart's turned inside-out. Rather than showcase the real Fifteen Minute Bob warts and all, I pad my film with lingering sweeps of his songwriting paraphernalia:

Those scribbled cornflake-packet lyrics.

His mouth organ.

His long, sinuous fingers.

His Martin acoustic.

And the empty whisky bottle. Natch . . .

Between you and me, rustling up this promo was hardly rocket-science. Without playing a trumpet voluntary, for a novice director I've created something 'straightforward and artistic'.

That's how I describe 'North Star' in the email I fire off to Stewart. As I press SEND, the first fingers of dawn creep in and tap me on the shoulder.

So taking the phone off the hook en route, I sleepwalk to my room. Crawl into bed without undressing.

'If Dad's song gets the thumbs up, we're sorted. And Mum won't need to go to Vancouver.' Soon as I sink into my pillow these words I whisper to myself scroll gently inside my head like a proclamation in neon: *Mum won't need to go to Vancouver*.

This good news revolves. Actually, I force these scrolling words to lullaby me. I want them to send me to sleep with a happy thought, just like Mum used to do when I was small.

But oh dear, you know what happens when your mind and body craves rest, and you *force* your brain to switch off? Though you're wiped, you end up wired. Dozing in snatches if you're lucky. Tossing. Turning. Finally giving up on sleep – like I do three hours after lying down. That's when Barry and Smillie arrive and start kicking and thumping the front door for attention.

'All right. All right. Co-*ming*!' I stumble from bed. Headachy. Sour.

'Ooof! Looking a bit rough there, Ro.' By way of greeting Barry sprays my face with muffin crumbs. Before I can remonstrate, Smillie donks my head with a trayful of carry-out coffees.

'Hair's insane. Lemme fix it.' Smillie 'fros me up. 'Been up all night with naughty Nettie, have you?'

Too washed out to defend anyone's honour, I trail Barry and Smillie to the sitting room where they settle in at the computer.

'Make yourselves at home, why don't you –' I begin,

but Barry waggles me a warning finger, his face flaring blue from the reflected light of the monitor.

'No offence, Ro, but don't go off on one, eh? We're here to work. If you wanna be useful, howz about telling Bladester we've brought breakfast.'

'Yeah, don't go off on one all hoity-toity Captain Superbrain – bugger me!' Smillie's half way through one of his random insults when the opening bar of 'Story of My Life' starts playing. 'Half a million hits now!' he taps the screen with the cappuccino he's been waving in dismissal at me. 'And check the comments: *"Luv luv luv vid."*, *"When ya giggin', mate?"*, *"Wanna see more, Tiffany. Lotz more xxxxx."* Well let's oblige de lady, Baz?'

Instead of pissing off as requested, I let Smillie open his stolen footage of myself and Nettie and play it through. While he and Barry snigger over the jumpy nonsense they filmed, I'm able to fortify myself with Dad's Danish and Americano before I pounce. Snatch the mouse. Delete all trace of their handiwork.

'Oi. Get Bladester we said, not ruin *this* while we're editing.' Before Smillie's even had the chance to think of squaring up to me, my hand grips his shoulder, pinning him to his chair.

'I'm not getting Dad yet. He'll be starting his new job today. Doing *this*.' I click the mouse. Open my film of 'North Star'.

I wish I could report that everything was Happy Ever After.

That Barry devours every second of my directorial debut. Then pumps my hand and tells me:

'Wow, Rory. *Your* film's light years better than that shit of ours. Sorry, mate.'

Instead of this:

'You're an up-tight, narrow-minded, supercilious fucking knob-end killjoy sometimes, Ro, who thinks you're better than the only two mates you've got thanks to your fucking smartarse attitude . . .'

While Barry's busy spitballing expletives at me, Smillie lets actions speak louder than words and launches himself at me like some *Reservoir Dogs* psycho. Borderline fatal his assault is. And not only to the video disc of 'North Star' which he snaps in my face with a sadistic flourish.

Barry has to forget he's in the huff to free me from one of those ninja holds that compress vital arteries.

'Shit, Ro, you're frothin'. I didn't mean what I said

back there,' Barry admits once he's rescued me from Smillie and we're both locked in my bathroom. 'No wonder Smiler's stoked, but. Cuz wiping our film's outa line. We're doing this for Bladester, not you. Well, not *directly* for you, though . . . well. We thought it might . . . y'know . . .'

Barry circles his arm about, his gesture taking in the tiled walls, gaping like neglected teeth, clogged with greyed grout.

And the ceiling: Saggy. Flaking. Our toilet with string for a handle, and a broken seat you lift from where it's propped against the bath if you fancy a warm crap . . .

'Oi. What's this new video of Bladester singing that we don't know about?' Smillie pummels at the door, but inside the bathroom, I contemplate my world through Barry's eyes.

'Oi, Baz. Rory's gone behind our backs.' Smillie agitates the door handle so roughly, the knob on my side clatters to the floor. 'He's emailing some guy in America. 'Bout Bladester.'

'Whassis?' Instead of fiddling to replace the broken handle, Barry brandishes it in my face. 'New song, eh?'

I try to explain. I do.

'*I* was helping Dad too. And Mum.'

Barry's having none of it. 'Top of the class, mate.'

From the pinch of his fingers on my collar while he frogmarches me to the computer, I suspect Barry's finished feeling sorry for me, a suspicion confirmed when I bleat, 'You're *really* hurting me,' and he tightens his grip.

'You've hurt *us*, mate.'

27
MUM ON THE WARPATH

So this is the chummy scene greeting Mum: I'm still in Barry's chokehold, while he and Smillie glower into the freeze-frame of Dad on screen and mutter darkly about what a tosser I am. Happening on such a cuddly tableau you'd think Mum – given her medical background – would at least ask Barry to release her son and heir. But no:

'Following Simon's footsteps after all?' She lays into me with the rolled-up newspaper she's carrying. 'No, no, keep a hold of him there. Tight –' Mum instructs Barry when he instinctively manoeuvres in front of me.

'Mrs Ryan, maybe talking's better –'

'Not when I'm trying to drum sense into this –'

WHACK

'– *eejit.*'

Barry ducks.

'I thought that fellow with the teeth was one of Simon's hangers-on, but he was a feckin' reporter, wasn't he, Rory?'

WHACK.

'And now all the nurses are watching you jiggling about daft on the internet –'

'What?' Barry and Smillie's eyebrows arch in unison.

WHACK.

'And all this time I thought you were going to be an *engineer* –'

WHACK. WHACK.

'Nurses are all wanting tickets for some tour –'

'Hot nurses, Baz! Phoaw! Love it!'

Ignoring Smillie's remark, Mum keeps whacking.

'Rory, I thought you'd more sense than to copy your ***Dad***.'

To my relief, Mum's final wallop is so energetic, her weapon flies from her hand. Though I don't mean relief because Mum's hurt me. She hasn't. But what *is* painful, is seeing Mum lash out. She's never, *ever* hit me. Never needed to, and I know her rage is fuelled by disappointment. That hurts more than a million whacks.

'Mum, you've got this wrong –' I extend my hand in appeal, but Mum flicks my whole arm away.

'Explain this then.' When she unfurls the newspaper, I reel from the photograph she smacks with the back of her hand. Feel like I've been socked in the jaw.

'No way,' Smillie peals. 'There's you snoggin' Annette.'

' "**Story of his Life: Fifteen Minute Kiss for Online Music Sensation**." Amazin'!' Barry jabs a finger under each word of the photo's caption. 'Rock Sensation Fifteen Minute Bob and mystery companion,' he reads, 'celebrate his download success. *Download success?* Smiler, if nurses are talking about a tour, we musta made the *nextbigthing* chart. Magic –'

'Magic?'

Mum couldn't have wiped the grins off Barry and Smillie any faster if she'd given them enemas without a local.

'Rory, if I'd known *this* was . . . honest to God . . . we'd have upped sticks years ago. Australia. Canada . . .' Pinching the corner of the paper like there's a turd on it, her eyes sweep our mismatched furniture, shabby curtains, tatty carpet. Her distaste is far more intense than Barry's when he perched on my bath, taking a similar inventory.

'I've only stuck things out because you seemed settled. Doing well. Decent mates. But behind my back –' Mum sinks into the chair at the computer. 'You're no different to –' She taps the frozen image of Dad on screen; the final frame of my film. His head's dipped over his guitar. Hair tumbling his face. Mum sighs at him like it's perfectly normal for his image to pop up whenever she wants to berate him.

'Though at least Simon *grafted* at the music.'

Mum's directing her remarks towards me, though she's really addressing Dad.

'Simon's *so* talented, but look how the music business screwed him up. Screwed us all. So why he'd encourage you when he knows how I feel . . .' Mum's eyes cut from the monitor. They narrow on me.

'You don't even dance. You can't carry a tune in a bucket –'

Before Mum becomes any more critical Barry chips in.

'Actually, Mrs Ryan –' he taps the snap of me and Nettie. '*We* put Rory on the internet behind his back. It wasn't him. And it was to help Mr Ryan –'

Mum ignores Barry, shooing him from her line of sight to leave her an undisturbed view of Dad. 'Why would you turn Rory's head? Haven't you given your son enough feckin' hang-ups?' she asks the computer.

Whoa!

Even if the squirmy glance I swear Barry and Smillie trade is my paranoia, it's time to nip Mum's reflections in the bud. She's veering dangerously close to dishing the dirt on my rocking phase, sleepwalking phase . . . Bedwetting follows.

Give them their due, Barry and Smillie seem as squirmy about Mum's bean-spilling as I'm feeling. Well Barry is.

'Word with Bladester,' he mouths at me as he edges offski. Whisks Smillie into the hall with him.

'Cringe, Baz. Thought *my* folks had the edge on messin' up their kids –' Smillie's stage-whisper is so loud, Barry's pathetic coughing fit masks nothing. Mum doesn't react, though. Something else is finally bothering her.

'What's Simon doing on the computer anyway? Looks wrecked.' She hovers her hands over the keyboard. 'How do you delete again?'

'No. Wait –'

As Mum clicks the mouse, the screen comes to life. Or rather, Fifteen Minute Bob comes to life.

'So this is how love feels,

When you've found your true North Star . . .'

Dad's voice wells from the speakers, his melody swirling through the flat. Finally Mum's quiet. And for as long as Dad's song plays, she remains so. Hands propping her chin. Just listening.

But don't get me wrong. I *specifically* didn't say Mum hears Dad's song all the way through.

She doesn't.

That would be *far* too conventional a way to close a chapter in Ryan Family Life. Think about it: In reality, scenes never fade neatly into the sunset. New stuff overlaps. Noisy stuff. Silly stuff. Stuff involving other people . . .

In this case Barry. Smillie. Dad. They're waiting in the wings. Also hearing 'North Star' properly for the first time.

Some of it.

Enough of it send one of them doolally.

Guess who?

28

THE NEW YESTERDAY

'Freak out! I'm Paul McCartney.'

Obviously, a former Beatle hasn't wandered into our skanky flat. Throwing peace signs.

And *obviously* the mentalist proclaiming, 'I've dreamed my new "Yesterday"!' is Dad.

'Wow, I *am* Paul McCartney. Freak *out*,' he persists. Until Mum seizes his wrists.

'Simon. What on earth have you taken now?'

Mum's tone remains nursery-teacher calm. Even when Dad's flailing arms catch her chin. Of course she's used to nutters lashing out left, right and centre at Casualty. Dad's behaviour is probably pretty tame by Saturday night standards in a big city A&E.

'Lemme go. Gotta write down my song. I've just dreamed it. Listen, Ria. It's for you –'

Wrenching free of Mum, Dad freezes in the middle of the hall, his boggly stare passing through her and upwards. As if he's seeing lyrics inscribed on the cornice, Dad takes a deep breath. Opens his mouth. Unfortunately nothing comes out. Even when Dad's eyes squint so tight they disappear, and his mouth pulls shapes that put me in mind of Barry's guppy, he doesn't produce one note.

'*Man*.'

Dad smacks the heel of his hand off his forehead.

'Stop it, Simon.' Mum's wince betrays enough anxiety to creep Barry, and then Smillie out from behind the kitchen door.

'Hey, Bladester –'

'Take it easy,' they flank my dad. As Barry pats his knobbled shoulder I feel my friend watching me. Awkward for me. Uncomfortable.

'But I've lost my song. Dreamed it like McCartney dreamed "Yesterday". Man, I'd words *and* music –'

Dad's on his haunches now, still thudding his head against his hand.

'It was so good –'

'Simon, do you want me to phone someone to take you away?' Mum's recovered her matron's composure. She's nodding. Slowly, like she's trying to hypnotise an admission out of Dad. 'Think you've been at the mushrooms again,' she sing-songs. 'Remember the visions last time? The rabbits?' Still nodding, Mum's level with Dad on the carpet. They way they kneel face to face reminds me of the wedding scene in *Romeo and Juliet*, only there's nothing remotely romantic about the way Mum dives at Dad. Begins to search his pockets.

'You'll be telling me Mick Jagger's swinging round next,' she sighs, flicking up Dad's arms. Running swift hands over his flanks. When she twitches her nostrils over Dad like a sniffer dog – 'Whisky for starters, from the stink off you' – Smillie actually groans. Looks away.

I feel humiliated for Dad too, seeing him manhandled like this by his own wife.

I hope he's unaware how pathetic he looks, letting Mum prod him as if he's packing weapons of mass destruction instead of a tune buried deep in his hangover.

While Mum's still frisking away, and Barry and Smillie are hovering in the background not quite knowing what to do with themselves, I slope off to the computer. My plan is to gather everyone round, casually enquire, 'Did your "Yesterday" sound like this, Dad?'

Then play 'North Star': *TA DA!*

Then I'll multiply the Good News: 'By the way, a record company's nibbling.'

And put Mum's mind at rest: 'You don't need to move to Canada after all.'

Yes, that's The Plan.

But alas, as a certain Scottish poet-songwriter with his finger on the pulse of the human condition and – coincidentally – the same first name as the legendary Blade himself once said: '*The best laid plans of well-meaning sons gang aft agley.*' Or something close.

Dad's Reveal, in other words, turns out to be more of an inconvenience than a triumph.

Smillie saunters into the sitting room with the enthusiasm of a bloke who's been asked to watch magnolia paint dry in an old folk's home when I call, 'Come in, everyone. You need to watch this.'

'Wassup?' he sigh-cum-yawns without glancing up from his mobile. 'Your mum's a bit tied up.'

Mum only half appears, jooking her head round the door. She has Dad propped against her like they're joined at the hip. As if! When she sees me at the computer, she about turns.

'Pet, if it's a school report, later, eh?'

Cuz it's hardly the best time, Ro, Barry's pursed mouth semaphores, his eyebrows clearly quizzing *d'you really need your mum's attention this* ***minute?*** Arms folded, head *just* shaking and no more, Barry watches me herding Mum and Dad back into the room. While I'm sitting them both in front of the computer, Barry glares at me with naked incomprehension. I press PLAY anyway.

'Look.' I shake Dad's arm for ages till he focuses on the screen and stops mumbling.

'Dad, you didn't dream your "Yesterday" after all.'

Oh, how epic it would be to report how my video fades to rapturous applause:

Encore!

Bravo!

Well done, sweetheart!

Awesome, Einstein!

But 'North Star' debuts to silence . . .

Well, almost.

Mum either hiccupps or sobs during the final chorus. This coincides with the moment in the song where Dad's voice soars and breaks. By luck, when I filmed this, my camera was zoomed as close to Dad's face as I could go, so my lens mapped every wrinkle and crevice and whisker and crow's foot before Dad's head sank. Between you and me, I thought it was a very powerful piece of *cinema verité*. Maybe Mum was thinking the same. At any rate, her voice turns as choky as it does whenever I tell her I've won the Science prize again.

'Simon,' she punches her chest as if there is a clump of words stuck or something. No one else reacts. I don't actually think Barry or Smillie *move* although, to be honest, I'm only properly watching Dad.

'Whhhhhhh,' he exhales. You'd think he'd been under water, holding his breath for too long. When the phone begins ringing in the hall, only his eyes slide towards the sound.

So I jump up.

'I'll get it.'

Mum's at my heels.

'Well?' I ask, smiling at her, polishing my nails on my shirt. 'No mushrooms this time, eh?'

I'm expecting my smile to be returned. And I'm *definitely* expecting Mum to wait to hear who's ringing like she always does. But she scuttles into her bedroom without so much as a glance at me.

'Mum?'

So although I automatically lift the receiver – 'Hello?' and hear, 'Stewart for Simon Anthony' – my heart follows Mum.

*Is she **crying**? Why?* is all I'm thinking, so when the voice on the line prompts, 'You there, Simon?', I feel as if I've connected to a parallel galaxy.

'Y . . . yes, I'm here Stewart.'

My reply's distracted. Well, I'm confused. Dad's song, rather than uplift anyone, has created an atmosphere so downbeat, I feel like I'm in one of those dreams where everything's familiar but out of kilter. I know I should be paying attention to Stewart telling me, 'Simon, we're blown away with "North Star",' but I'm drawn to the silence crackling from Mum's room like white noise.

Worry sours the sweetness of Stewart chuckling, 'We gotta jet you and FMB Stateside.' *What's the matter with Mum?* I'm thinking. *And why doesn't Dad say **anything** about* 'North Star' *yet? And when . . . **how*** – my stomach cramps and knots – *do I admit I'm a different 'Simon' to the one Stewart dealt with yesterday? And why don't I hear Barry and Smillie speaking?*

Frankly, my mates' silence is so out of character I'm worried our dodgy gas fire might be leaking carbon monoxide. I'm actually lowering the receiver on Stewart to check what's happening in the sitting room when – relief – *North Star* begins playing again.

Distracted, I forget I'm on a transatlantic call, my ear straining to try and catch what Dad's mumbling instead.

'Simon, hey, I'm getting dead air.' I jump when Stewart's tone suddenly sharpens.

'. . . As I say, the track's awesome, but *no one* sees that video you sent. It's wiped already . . .'

'What? Y'don't like the video?' I gulp. *My film? What's wrong with it?*

'Have you *watched* it, Simon?'

Stewart's bray is so blaring that even Dad can hear him. As he opens the sitting room door, calling over his shoulder to Barry and Smillie, 'Well, my track sounds fine. Pity the dude singing on the video looks 'bout ready to meet up with Hank, Roy and Elvis,–' he catches Stewart using this businessman name.

'Hey. If that's for Sim-on,' Dad cups his hands over the mouthpiece and hollers all the way to America, 'I ain't here.'

'Hello? Simon? Is Bob there too? *Our* Bob? Fifteen Minute?' Stewart puzzles while I whisk the receiver from

Dad's reach. I press it so hard to my chest I can feel Stewart's words vibrating my ribcage.

'Hey, if Bob's there, put him on the line, Simon. Lemme say hi –'

'*Dad* –' I whisper urgently, wielding the receiver. 'This call's about your song.' I make a thumbs up, but Dad blanks me. Reverses into his bedroom. Before the door closes, I glimpse Mum. She's perched on the mattress. Huddled in her outdoor coat.

'Ria,' says Dad.

And Mum turns her face to the wall.

'. . . And, I'm sorry, but whatever wiseass thought FMB fans wanna sit watching an old soak miming . . .'

Returning to Stewart, I catch him mid-rant and immediately clamp the voice against my chest again.

Shit.

Bomb goes my plan for unmasking the real Fifteen Minute Bob.

Stewart hates my video. ***Shit!*** I gulp, staring at Mum and Dad's door. *And where's Mum going?*

'– So we sign FMB,' Stewart's in full flight when I gingerly return the phone to my ear, 'then reshoot our promo. Wanna see Bob singing under a heap of *stars.*

You get it, Simon? *Stars*. You lovin' it?'

I got it. I wasn't lovin' it.

'And we make a mini-movie. *Love Story* kinda thing: Preppies hooking up in astronomy class. Geddit? North Star? Astronomy? Course, we'll hire us some OC eye-candy. Leggy. Bulimic. Pretty-boy vampire lead. *High School Musical* meets *First Blood* with balls on –'

Stewart's lost me now.

'You still there?' he calls. 'Lemme tell ya, our creatives're kicking up so many smokin' ideas the Fire Department's on standby.'

I try to parrot Stewart's laughter.

Can't.

Not when the *true* source of *anything* he plans is a door-thickness away, the pleading cadences in Dad's voice finding no harmony in Mum's droned replies.

Stewart ignores the dead air between us this time.

'So, we film these hot kids makin' out, getting' down, fallin' out – you get the picture?'

'*What? Shitty painting-by-numbers schmaltz. An insult to the rawness of my dad's song,*' I hear myself splutter.

Unfortunately not aloud. Because my speaking voice is too busy stammering.

'Actually Stewart, "North Star" is not about falling in love. Or astronomy.'

Not that Stewart hears me.

'Hey, Simon?' he shouts over me, 'Still with me? I gotta tell you this. Session man just swung by my office. Guy's a Nashville vet. Played with old Bob Blade himself on the *Chief Sequoia and Long Jaw* album back in '66. He heard me spinning "North Star". Just the song. No pictures. Still with me, Simon?'

'Still with you,' I reply although I've stopped breathing. *Someone who backed Bob Blade has heard Dad? That's one degree of separation. That's awesome . . .*

'Anyway, I tell this old timer FMB's some cute Brit wunderkid, and he ain't buying.' Stewart hoots. 'Showed him our boy singing "Story of My Life" on the web: 'Check it out; just a knock-kneed puppy-fat kid, still wet behind the ears.' Old timer *still* ain't buying.' Stewart affects an aged warble: '*No dude sings pain like that 'fore he's done some livin' and losin'*.'

'Y'said this session man played with Blade? *Bob* Blade? *The* Bob Blade? The "Hey Starfish Woman" Bob Blade?' I raise my voice over Stewart's laughter.

'And he liked my dad's song?'

Ooops.

There's no dubiety about what I've just asked Stewart. What I've revealed.

This time the dead air carries the chill of the Atlantic.

'Pardon me?' Stewart's voice is Coke laced with vinegar. 'D'you just say your *dad's* song? Dad as in pop?'

'I-I did.' *Gulp. Deep breath.* 'Thing is, that bloke on the video of "North Star" is Fifteen Minute Bob. And he's my dad. It's him dancing in "Story of My Life", too. He wrote it. *And* he's the real Simon Anthony . . .'

I'm holding myself so tense during these admissions, my back goes into spasm. This bears out what Mum's always said about telling the truth and shaming the devil being painful! Up until now I assumed she meant *psychologically*. Coming clean to Stewart, however, hurts like stink. I'm bent double.

'Bit of a mix-up,' I wince, adding quickly, before Stewart has the chance to snap more than, 'You're telling me, bud.'

'But my dad's no fake.'

Well, what do I have to lose?

'His name's Blade, not Simon – well his *real* name's

Simon. Actually his real name's not actually Simon . . . it's Blade now . . . Point is, he's been a musician for thirty years. And trying to reach someone your level in the business forever,' I plough on, knowing how flattery *always* sweetens the audience in a debate.

As does positivity: 'And Dad's written *piles* of songs. You'd have albumsful if you signed him. *Please*, give him a break . . .'

Okay, so Bob Blade, poet and troubadour, I'm not. But, under the circumstances. I'm doing my best.

Especially with Smillie breathing down my neck now.

'Still on the blower talking dirty with Nettie?'

And Barry. 'You've some explaining to do, Ro.'

Oh. And in the midst of everything, Mum slips out with a suitcase.

'Call you,' she promises me, holding an imaginary phone to her ear. Doesn't say goodbye.

'Dad! Where's Mum going?' I'm panicking before Stewart concludes our conversation with a frosty, 'Need to take a raincheck on Fifteen Minute Bob.'

'Job interview for Vancouver tomorrow. In London,' she says.

Dad stumbles across the hall like our flat is collapsing

and he can't keep his footing.

'Didn't you tell her why you wrote "North Star"?' my voice rises.

Before Dad's done shrugging the words, 'Think Ria's washed her hands this time, man,' I'm down two flights of stairs faster than I can recite the Table of Elements.

'Mu-um!'

Apart from a taxi turning the corner, our street's empty.

'Mate.'

That's all Barry says when he joins me on the pavement.

Smillie just kneads my upper arm with his knuckles.

Without any of their usual banter, they flank me till I'm ready to give up hoping Mum might reappear.

'Better head up and get my work done,' I say eventually.

'Now?' Smillie raises one hand towards my sitting room window, his body turned in the direction Mum disappeared.

'Oi!' First of all Barry intercepts whatever inappropriate opinion Smillie's about to blurt with a 'zip-it' head-jerk.

Then he chucks my arm. 'You do whatever, mate.' His voice is soft. 'And if there's . . . y'know . . . *anything* . . .'

We both shrug, dropping our heads. And boy, am I grateful not to be looking into Barry's eyes. Mine are hot. Stinging. My vision swimmy. I squeeze my lids till the nippiness subsides. When I open my eyes again Smillie's turned away. I hear the delicate pitter of him texting.

'Want us to check on Bladester with you?'

Even as I shake my head, Barry's anticipating my answer.

'Okay. But remember, Ro: Phone. Stay. Eat. Talk. Wot mates like us are for.' He's backing along the street. 'Oh, and Bladester's new song . . . WOW, by the way. And your film –' he throws a sheepish thumbs-up, like he knows what he's trying to say is irrelevant right now but wants to leave me with something positive anyway. 'Take it that phone call was about . . .?'

'. . . How crap my film is.'

I'm almost grateful to have something less awkward than Mum bailing to discuss.

'Bigshot American record guy loved the song. Said Dad's image spoiled it, though. Doesn't want the package.'

'Bladester's image?' Barry's affronted. 'And he hated your film? But it was quality!'

Smillie's less upset. 'Point is, he dug Bladester's *song*?' He blings me a grin. 'So we're still in business. Just delete your shit. Baz 'n' me'll do a better film –'

'Nah.' I take the precaution of having distance between Smillie and myself before admitting, 'The Stewart guy knows Dad's not me now. I'm kinda glad. We'd've been rumbled as soon as we went to America.' I'm surprised to feel myself close to snickering. 'He wanted us over there to make an album and –'

'America? You're joking me?'

The air I inhale suddenly tastes of Juicy Fruit and Smillie's fiery breath.

'Smiler,' Barry has to hook him back. 'Leave it for now.'

'Leave it full stop.' I take advantage of Barry's promise to do anything for me. 'Don't involve me any more. *I* can't make a record. Don't play guitar. Can't sing. Can't even mime. You know what I'm like playing that Beatles Rock Star game on your Wii –'

'You don't have to *sing,* dumb-butt.' Smillie addresses me in the most offensive spaz voice I've ever heard him use. 'We just get you and Bladester to America. Then switcheroo. Stick Bladester in the studio disguised as you. Slap some makeup on him. Big shades. A mask. Mickey Jacko got away with it for years. Anything's possible if you want it enough . . .'

'But *I* don't want that. Neither would Dad. It's a fake way to be famous. Anyway –' my eyes are stinging again – 'how can we swan off anywhere *now*? With my mum . . .'

'Sure.' Barry steers me clear of Smillie. Without asking if I want an escort this time, he walks me upstairs. Steers me into the sitting room.

'Is it okay if I copy Bladester's new song?' He isolates his memory stick keyring. Jabs it into a USB port on the computer.

'Your mum'll come back,' Barry tells me while he's saving my song to his dongle. He pats my arm. 'Prob'bly,' he adds as he leaves the flat. Not very confidently.

29

CIRCLING THE SQUARE

But Mum did come back.

Well, she'd packed enough clothes for a couple of overnights. No winter coat. No passport. She needed both. The Vancouver contract was for at least six months. So a week after her interview, she came home. It was late morning. She must have assumed I was at school. I can't believe Mum would have organised for a shipping crate to arrive when it did otherwise. Salt. Wounds. Rub etc.

This is weeks and weeks ago, by the way.

And actually, it was Nettie who let the carriers in. Ever since Smillie texted her while I was outside the flat with him and Barry the night Mum finally walked away from Dad – and me – Nettie's been popping over on a daily basis. Within half an hour that first time. Still wet and shivery, pretending not to be worried about the bollocking her old man would dish her for coming back to see me instead of doing her homework, she perched on my bed just listening while I blurted what had happened with Stewart. Then about 'North Star'. How even though a genuine vintage Bob Blade session man loved Dad's song, it didn't stop Mum following her head.

When I told Nettie that, she gave me the biggest hug I'd had since I last woke from a bad dream with Mum's arms round me. Wet me right through to the skin, did Nettie's hug. Warmed me to the core at the same time.

The next day when she came to see why I hadn't made school, Nettie brought me and Dad a cake she'd baked. Plus classwork. Don't know what she'd told Doc Martin and Miss Sweet, but they both sent notes:

Just do what you can, Rory

There are far more important things in life than passing exams.

Take care of yourself.

And if there's any way I can help.

That was the gist of both messages. Which surprised me. Not just because I've always assumed the only important thing in Doc Martin's life is Physics. I was also surprised that despite a massive age-gap, the two messages were almost identical. And identical to the gist of what Barry keeps telling me too: Look after yourself, Ro. No one's expecting you to be bloody swotting any more!

I admit, I've given serious thought to what Doc and Sweetie wrote. Their notes meant nearly as much as Nettie's cake. But *that* I couldn't touch. Well, in the days after Mum left, all I was eating were my fingernails. Dad wasn't eating full stop. Just drinking systematically through anything stashed in his den.

Anyway, by the time Nettie opens our door to a packing crate and two couriers, she's stopped making excuses for visiting me. She just comes over and cuddles into me while I scroll the internet dealing with enquiries about Fifteen Minute Bob:

Where's he touring?

When's the album out?

Does he have a fan club?

Ever since Barry dongled my 'shit' film, then posted it without editing on various non-mainstream music sites featuring raw bluesy folk, there's been – I'm NOT exaggerating – *tens* of thousands of hits. Worldwide. In fact, both Dad's songs are on viral charts all over cyberspace.

'*"FMBob. Loo so Lock."*' I'm reading out this comment from Japan in a silly accent, when scuffling at the front door distracts Nettie enough to leave my side.

'For God's sake, Simon. A schoolgirl!' I hear Mum's voice before I see her. She obviously doesn't recognise Nettie from the newspaper snog-snap that upset her so much. Mum just clocks short skirt, long hair, pretty face. Assumes the worst.

'Hi, Mum! Dad's working.' I hurry out to referee before Mum's tongue runs away with her. 'He's a security guard. Started a few days ago. This is *my* friend, Nettie. She's in my Physics class.'

'But I'm rubbish at it.' Nettie's trying to muster a smile. Tricky when Mum's eyes are spiking her with suspicion.

'And what are you both doing here when you should be at school?'

'*Doin'?*' The eruption of snorts from the carriers on the landing reminds Mum she has an audience – '*What you think they kids'r doin', missus? Playin' Scrabble?*'

While she's arranging the uplift of her packing case

with these sniggering blokes, Nettie slips offski.

'Aren't you going to school too, pet?' Mum suddenly less prickly when it's just us two in the flat.

I flick my hand at the civvies I'm wearing. 'Dun't look like it.' My voice is gruff. Cold. Accusing. I don't mean to be nasty though. Shit. Mum looks rougher than I've *ever* seen her: eyes red-rimmed, hair lank, skin wan. *I don't want you to go to Canada, Mum. Even for six months,* my normal voice pleads. But the words won't exit my mouth.

'You're leaving tomorrow?' I face Mum across the packing case, gripping the top of it with both hands.

'It's a fantastic job. Not for long. Time'll whiz past. And it'll make such a difference cashwise. For both of us. But listen – and I'm not nagging – go to school, love. It's only weeks till your –'

'Like you care!'

Forget Mum's reaction. The venom in that remark makes *my* cheeks throb, temples pulse, eyes nip. Thinking about them even *now,* when everything's moved on; remembering how they made Mum wince that last day the flat was her home, I know I'll be wishing I could take back those words I spat forever. My verbal poison drains Mum's lips of colour. Must have gone straight to her heart. Her reply was no more than a whisper.

'I'm only doing this because I have to, Rory. I'm sorry. Sometimes things can't stay the way they are. I can't rely on your dad. We know that. Life's got to change.'

Mum edges round the packing case towards me. So I use it to keep my distance. If you didn't know the circumstances, you'd think we were playing tig.

Not Endgame.

Mum reaching out. Me, sidestepping a touch that would crumble me.

'It's only six months, Rory.'

'It's ages.'

'But you'll be out when your exams finish. That's just weeks away. Spend the summer. They're giving me a lovely apartment.'

'But what about Dad?'

'What *about* Dad?'

'He's got a real job.'

'Good for him.'

'You wanted him to get a job. He's done it. And everyone *loves* that song he wrote you.'

'I'm pleased. It's a grand song.'

'No, but Mum, people want to *buy* it. Stuff's happening. He's signed. He's making an album.'

'I'm delighted.'

'So you don't really need to leave.'

'It's only six months.'

'*Ages.*'

'It'll be great weather when you come out.'

'Can Dad come too?'

'We'll see. Sounds like he might be busy . . .'

Looking back, I should just have kept Mum playing tig along the sides of that packing crate. We could have gone round in circles for six months. Or at least till Dad came home. So Mum could see he was trying his best.

But she'd made her mind up.

30
GUDDLING

And now it's *so* long since Mum came back that day. I've stopped feeling angry about her. Just feel sad. Some days without her pass more easily than others. Though by 'easily' I only mean *less* painfully. Till Mum split, I never realised how missing someone you love physically *hurts*. Cramping your ribs, aching your throat, throbbing the back of your eyes . . .

Even with months gone by, I *still* have this ache. Feels like scar tissue forming, tightening, tugging. And it's always, *always* there. In the background of whatever I'm doing, whether it was my A levels (all done and dusted, by the way; a breeze compared to learning to live without Mum) or guddling with Dad, pair of us trying to cook something between us without incinerating it, or calling Nettie:

'Listen, can you eat chicken if it's pink in the middle?'

Interestingly, the ache only numbs a little while I'm

being Fifteen Minute Bob's roadie, lugging guitars and amps in and out our van. Making sure Dad is set up: Jack Daniel's in a paper cup. Set-list. Mouth organs . . . I suppose I'm just too busy to notice I'm hurting. I can be almost pain-free while I humph Dad's gear, adjusting it to whatever venue he's booked to play.

Yes. That's what I said: *Booked* to play . . .

So many gigs since Mum left, Dad was actually able to *quit* being a security guard. We toured pubs and Student Unions to begin with. Then bigger venues: Small town halls, the new band circuit. But lately Fifteen Minute Bob's name is cropping up on flyers for music festivals. Have a look. And OK, I know he's still one of the names you scan once you've read who's headlining, and printed twenty times smaller than The Killers or Kings of Leon. But Fifteen Minute Bob's there, isn't he?

Whenever I remark on our change of fortune Dad shrugs and lays me some Bob Blade wisdom. About how Bob said something somewhere about how everyone who sticks in and slugs it out gets their chance in the end.

'Guess this is just my time rollin' round at last.'

I don't share Dad's nonchalance. His growing cult

status gobsmacks me. I mean after years of never getting a look-in, Dad has fans crushing the stage, for Chrissakes. Footstamping for the live version of this wrecked internet viral bloke with his raw songs. People are wearing *his* gnarly face on their chests. So that Stewart bloke was way wrong: Old Landy might be a pathetic father and such a crap husband that Mum finally skedaddled across the Atlantic, but there's no denying his musical talent is real. Dad's never going to have the youth or beauty to turn him mainstream, but he's finally being recognised for the way he sings and writes and plays.

So that's what I find so brilliantly stunning about Dad's 'overnight success after thirty years in the doghouse, man' as he keeps joking.

You're making it despite being yourself.

That's what I think every time Dad strolls onstage with his guitar over his shoulder. Toasts his audience with the throwback cliché, 'Great to be here, man.'

From the wings, I watch Dad and watch his audience watching him, all mouthing his lyrics. In those moments I feel breathless with pain as well as pleasure.

See, I keep wishful-thinking Mum was beside me. *Finally* seeing Dad doing what he always wanted to do.

Sounding like he wants to sound. No concessions. True to himself.

Like Bob Blade had always been, through every musical phase in his own life and despite the critics.

Sometimes I wish so hard for Mum to be with me, I feel the heat of her arm against my side. Smell her perfume. Catch her shadow. It's horrible, I'm telling you, missing someone *so* much your mind conjures them up. You think you glimpse them out the corner of your eye. Gasp. Turn. No one. It's bloody horrible.

The Power of Yearning on the Human Psyche: *there's* a PhD waiting to be written.

Though not a subject I'll be tackling.

Nah. Too airy-fairy for an Applied Scientist like myself. And a bit too near the knuckle this weather. Anyway, my brain's still hard-wired for Engineering, though not the branch I'd all mapped out through school.

Sorry, Mum.

Since I started working round Dad, I've lost interest in reading Physics and Engineering at St Andrews or Herriot-Watt. Fancy Sound Engineering instead.

Working with Dad and other musicians in the studio, I'm totally intrigued that techie skills as precise and scientific as the ones you use on a mixing desk can influence how individual listeners *feel*. What a mind-blowing power for an engineer to have at his fingertips!

But I won't be doing anything about anything. Not for at least a year. Maybe longer. *Shhh. Maybe never*. Depends . . . on how long Dad needs me to roadie for him and Mickey and rest of band FMB . . .

Barry's delighted with my decision, of course. Reckons I should forget uni altogether. He wants us to go into partnership.

'Your brains, my business sense. It's a dream ticket, Ro.'

For months I've been fobbing Barry off. See, Barry wants me to join his music company. *Hera,* it's called, after his favourite Blade song. Poor Barry. Since Hera is one of Mr Masterton's speculative ventures, naming it is the only executive decision Barry's made so far. No disrespect to Barry but I'd hate to answer to a hardbitten honcho like his old man. Mr M doesn't give a flying crap about Health and Safety or employee rights. I suppose that's why he can afford to upgrade his Mercs twice a year, and set his unqualified-for-anything-else son up as a Musical Svengali.

But Good Luck to Barry. He's solid and I'm delighted he's sitting pretty with his recording studio, suite of offices, and sweet PA that Smillie's on a mission to deflower. Street-smart, never book-smart, Barry's in his element at last, trawling the club scene and internet virals for fresh talent. Loving it. But scouting new bands, then trying to manage and auto-tune them while they cram a lifetime's worth of excess into *their* fifteen minutes, is not my idea of a fulfilling career.

'Still doing my roadie,' I keep telling Barry when he begs me to oversee his recording studio permanently. I don't want to risk our friendship by telling him I'll never take up my seat on the board.

I can't afford to lose a mate like him. Not while me and Dad are still guddling, trying to figure the most basic elements of getting along.

By getting along, I'm not talking about 'getting along' in our personal relationship. I mean basic survival: Eating properly. Paying utility bills so there's power when we come home from Glenrothes Town Hall at three in the morning needing hot showers and a cuppa.

In *personal* relationship terms, although things are

complex between me and Dad, they could be a lot worse than they are . . . Have been.

Funny. Till Mum left, and me and Dad fell into working together, we never talked. About anything. We just sniped. Picked away at our differences. Used Mum as a go-between if we had to. But now that we spend all day in each other's company, we talk constantly. About work, that is:

OK, how did the last gig really go?

Did the band play well?

Do the audience like the new songs?

Did the Bob Blade covers medley pass muster?

However, me and Dad still don't *talk* talk.

Not like I talk to Nettie. Cutting to the chase whether we're face to face or – mostly these days – on a phone, on the road, between gigs.

Mum. That's what me and Nettie talk about. How much Dad and I miss her. And about what's going to happen when her six months in Canada are up. We talk about where I'll live if I change my mind about going off to uni and want to come 'home' for the summer. And me and Nettie also talk about us. How we wish Dad would relax his 'No Skirt on Gigs' rule for even one night so

Nettie can join me backstage. Or wait up for me in our own hotel room . . .

Yes. Me and Dad confine our talk to work.

'You should hear yourselves: Venues, riders, Pro Tools,' Smillie complained when he and Barry interrupted the last Fifteen Minute Bob debriefing we were able to have in our own flat.

'Yeah. But at least Ro and Bladester are talking about *something* together. And Ro's finally acting his age and letting his hair down.' Barry 'fro-ed me up. I didn't mind though. It's not like I wear a side-parting any more. And as for his comment about acting my age . . . well, Barry's not the only one who's been making it.

Dad thinks so too. He remarks on this change in me every night we play.

'Okay, people. So I wanna dedicate this song to someone I never thought I'd need, or mind havin' about,' Dad tells his audience. Usually just when I'm scurrying into the spotlight to hand Dad the classical guitar he uses for his arrangement of a song Bob Blade released when he was in his early twenties. Nearly half a century ago. 'Workin' Man Collar Too Rough' the song's called. The lyrics could be about Bob Blade sloughing off his earnest folkie down-home persona and evolving as a musician and a man. But Dad *makes* them be about me, changing Bob Blade's original pronoun when he cocks his head to the wings and confides to hundreds and hundreds of strangers about how his son is finally acting a lot more like *that kid he didn't wanna be when he coulda, shoulda been that kid . . .*

I *think* he's paying me a compliment.

I take it as one anyway.

31
MY BACK PAGES

So. Yeah. I've come a long way from that Sixth Form Parents' Night.

Literally.

Seven months on and I'm in Vancouver. With Dad. And Mum. It's early spring. Crisp. Sunny. Beautiful. We're in Stanley Park, having a family day out. Isn't that lovely? Dad's idea: 'A gander at the aquarium. Bit of a cycle. Finish up with a sod-the-moolah lunch now I'm flush.'

Sounds too good to be true, doesn't it?

It is.

Only me and Mum are cycling. And forget lunch. After a textbook sex, drugs and rock'n'roll lost night to celebrate the end of his first North American tour, Dad's been propping up a magnolia tree groaning how he digs what Blade means when he sings 'all 'bout his universe throbbin' out nothin' but black an' ugly, maaan. Y'know?

In that song? 'Bout your chick, Einstein'. (I should explain here that Dad's talking about 'Losin' Nettie', a track off Bob Blade's recent *Still Breathin'; Keepin' On* with a chorus that even *I* like. And not just because I accidentally found a girl named after it.)

'Good old Simon. Wrecked on the first day he's bothered to organise,' Mum suddenly blurts after the pair of us have cycled abreast for a couple of miles.

'No wonder you like it here,' I change the subject, catching up Mum and her fancy trail bike at a totem pole she's stopped to admire.

'I *love* it, Rory. Everything's so healthy.'

Behind her shades I feel Mum's eyes resting on me, unshaven since I lost my razor in Amsterdam a week ago. Taking in the roadie combat shorts and Dad's Woodstock T-shirt, she sweeps her hand at the lagoon in front of us, and the cityscape beyond.

'Skiing, hiking, mountains, cycling, fishing, sailing, culture. This place has *everything*. Officially the best city in the world.'

Point made, Mum angles her neck so I can't see her face. 'You know, you could enrol in an engineering programme at the University of British Columbia. Get back on track.' Mum draws a big breath of Canadian air before she adds, 'And I'll sort you digs, if you're uncomfortable living with me and Randy.'

Yeah. Yeah. Yeah. So us Ryans are reunited. But this is real life remember, not some fairytale:

The End.

Ahhhhh.

As FMB sings in one of his new songs:

'Ain't no such thing as an all-round happy endin'

Someone always gotta sacrifice

Someone always gotta pay the price –'

Dad's right, isn't he? Jagger too: You *can't* always get what you want. Take Mum's situation. She's never done insisting, 'Life's grand here so.'

And on the surface it sure seems that way, bud!

Mum looks ten years younger for a start. Her skin glows, her eyes shine, her hair bounces about her face. She jogs every morning round this same track we're cycling.

A couple of months ago she left the flat she rented when she first arrived in Vancouver. Moved into an uptown condo. It has panoramic views over the Pacific.

A gym in the basement. The condo even comes with its own resident cardiologist.

Randy.

'Randy's such a lovely man, Rory. Don't you think?' Mum's asked this so often since me and her lovely man were introduced yesterday, I'm wondering if she's trying to convince herself as well as me she's done the right thing replacing Dad with a widower on the wrong side of sixty.

'Rory, isn't Randy lovely?'

Bloody hell! That was the *first* thing Mum asked when she brought New Guy backstage during Fifteen Minute Bob's final encore of the tour.

What could I say? When Mum whispered her question to me, I was *nearly* as shell-shocked as I knew Dad would be. Couldn't *believe* this suave, silver-haired wrinkler and *my* mum were . . . *all loved up.* ***Sleeping*** *together. Sister Ryan and this old Doc in his slacks and blazer* . . . unbelievable! To add insult to injury, Randy was almost the same vintage as a certain other Canadian 'cat' who'd been similarly devastating to my parents' helter-skelter marriage . . .

While my arm was being pumped within an inch of dislocation – 'So us fellow scientists finally meet!' – Dad was bidding eight hundred new West Coast fans farewell as they sang him offstage to the last chorus of 'North Star'.

'Hope my lady hears that, dudes. G'night!' he waved, bounding into the wings. Pumped. Elated. Straight into the biggest reality check of his life.

'Ria.'

'Hello, Simon.'

'Ria. Wow, angel, your hair. You look . . .'

'Simon. This is my friend –'

'Dr Randy Kochek. Good to meet you.'

For one bizarre moment my parents and Randy were linked: Dad's left hand cupping Mum's cheek while Randy manoeuvred himself between them. Bonecrushed Dad's long guitar-man fingers in his surgeon's grip. I noticed Mum's New Old Man held on to her like he was worried she might slip his grasp. Return to the Dark Side. Then, as cheers and footstomping from the auditorium swelled to such a pitch of anticipation I couldn't compute the significance of this scene any more, Randy drew Mum away. Thumbed his competition towards the chants of 'F.M.B! F.M.B! F.M.B!' until Dad seized the guitar I thrust into his hands. Stumbled back on stage.

*

So, who could blame Dad getting wasted last night? With a studio album set for release and a hard-graft tour that's earned Fifteen Minute Bob the reputation of *THE* live act worth catching should he come to a moderately sized venue near you, Dad probably believed he could just breeze into town. Win Mum back. Like some character in a song. Or a movie. Or a soap. Or on a white charger. Thought his success would impress her:

Didn't I tell you it would all work out one day, Ria?

Thought coming good as Fifteen Minute Bob would make up for over twenty shit years of real life . . .

But getting what you want carries penalties.

Anyway, that's the situation with my folks. Kaput. Even though I reckon something . . . love, whatever . . . *I* don't know, still sputters and glints like a tiny diamond in their personal dungheap of crap and hurt and history. Always will. That's true love, Nettie says. But as a functioning unit, they're beyond repair.

I'll stop discussing them now.

Don't want you quitting me on a downer.

'Gotta leave folk smiling.' That's what Dad tells the

band when they huddle-up before every gig.

So, here I am, taking Dad's advice. Who would have thought that? Or that Mr Perfect with life all mapped out would part company from you quite content to ride the thermals of a rock and roll band cruising at altitude because he doesn't know where he's going himself any more.

And he doesn't really care . . .

32
NUGGET

So. Time to leave you with that smile, I hope.

Well *I* smiled. Grinned. Cheered. Celebrated. Shimmied, à la FMB, believe it or not. At least I did once I'd sifted this sparkly nugget from the hysterical burble streaming out my mobile when I answered it in the middle of my last night in Vancouver.

'Ro! Ro! You're not going to *believe* this.' Barry's voice was so squealy, I thought some loopy FMB groupie was pranking me from the lobby. Lucky I didn't cut the call.

'Rory?' A less high-pitched voice took the phone.

'Nettie? *Nettie?* What you doing with Barry?'

'Ta da! I'm here too, sunshine?' Despite being time zones apart, Smillie's foghorn throbbed my fillings. 'How's it hanging? Guess what?'

'Wot?' It was four a.m. Less than two hours before I'd be waking Dad to start our journey home. In twenty-four hours Smillie could bellow me deaf in person with whatever it was he was blurting about Bob Blade. Not a word made sense over the tussle taking place down the line.

'Gimme the phone back, Smiler. *I* wanna tell him. Or Nettie should.'

'Piss off. We're his *mates*, Bazzer.'

'She's Rory's *girl* –'

''S'okay. You tell him, Barry. You're his best friend. And you know all Blade's songs off by heart anyway –'

'Okay then listen, Ro. We're in Manchester. Just seen Bob Blade in concert,' Barry's voice finally gasped.

'And it's freezing,' I heard Nettie pipe up in the background. She sounded more elated than she was last week, reading me and Dad the first UK review for Fifteen Minute Bob's album, *The New Kid*. (Four star, by the way.)

'Blade was *so* legend,' Barry continued. 'White Stetson on. Cool as fu–'

'– You've travelled all the way to Manchester for a Bob Blade gig?'

I was fully awake now.

'Found tickets on eBay. Place was full of Gandalfs in hearing aids. And old Bob coulda done with you behind the controls, Ro,' Barry chuckled. 'Sound was like marshmallows singing in a duvet –'

'Shit, but it was still Bob Blade live,' Smillie's excitement scattergunned Barry's criticism away.

'Too right, still Blade. He sang "Workin' Man's Collar", "Hey Starfish Woman", "Bride Ain't Never Gonna Get Wed", "Rudolph" off *The Christmas Album*, "Hera", just for me –'

'And "Losin' Nettie", Rory. It was amazing. That *chorus* broke my heart . . .' Suddenly *my* Nettie's voice was so close, I could feel her lips against my ear. 'Wish you were here.'

The hoarseness in Nettie's whisper gave me stomach cramp. Shivers. Homesickness. 'Nettie. Wait.' *Meet me at the airport* I wanted to tell her, but Barry was pressing.

'Listen. You gotta tell Bladester. Gotta tell him we've just seen Bob –?'

'Tell him yourself, Baz. We're home in twelve hours. Put Nettie back on, eh?'

'Just *listen*, Ro. *Please* –' Barry's voice drops. 'Bob sang "Lone Trails and Neverendin' Highways" as an encore, right? He changed the tempo, played this bluesy intro . . .'

'Fascinating,' I was yawning obviously. 'Bob Blade never sings a song the same way twice. Ever. Ever. Even *I* know that –'

I reckon Barry counted to ten here, because there was a bit of a silence. Eventually he sniffed. 'This news is actually for your dad, but his phone's off.' Barry's hurt simmered till I urged, 'Go on then.'

And that's when Barry told me how the real live legendary Bob Blade himself segued from *his* chorus to the hook of –

'"Story of My Life", Ro. Swear to God, Ro.'

'*What?*'

'Bob Blade SANG our Bladester's song.' Barry was shouting now. His voice had climbed an octave. 'And you know what –'

'The place went ballistic!'

Smillie couldn't contain himself. There was a scuffle before Barry could blurt.

'*Everyone* recognised it, Ro. "*Story of ma . . . story of ma . . .*" they were all singing along. With Blade. With *the* Bob Blade. Oh, man, Smiler'n'Nettie'n'me were screamin' how much we wished you were here. You *and* Bladester. Tellin' you, no joke, I was in tears –'

'Aw, mate. Thanks,' I just about managed to splutter.

Then I crossed the corridor. To wake Dad.

MORE GREAT STORIES BY CATHERINE FORDE

The Drowning Pond

Hey, guess what?
You're no one. Invisible.

But what if one day the glossy people noticed you, made you their friend...
And then changed their minds.

If you could get back in by picking on the weirdo new girl.
You would. Wouldn't you?

Fat Boy Swim

What would folks say if they discovered that big blob Kelly had one special talent and it involved food? God's sick joke that.

Cooking is Jimmy Kelly's secret gift. Bullied viciously at school, the kitchen is his haven.

But even he doesn't know his real secret. He can't start living, until he stops hiding.

And for older readers...

Skarrs

Danny-Boy's got his head shaved for Grampa Dan's funeral. Just to see their faces. Is he grieving? Too right.

Instead of sitting in this church, he could be away in his room. Skarrs pumping on the speakers.

The way Skarrs play, they could wake the dead.

See **www.egmont.co.uk** for information on these great books and many others!

EGMONT PRESS: ETHICAL PUBLISHING

Egmont Press is about turning writers into successful authors and children into passionate readers – producing books that enrich and entertain. As a responsible children's publisher, we go even further, considering the world in which our consumers are growing up.

Safety First
Naturally, all of our books meet legal safety requirements. But we go further than this; every book with play value is tested to the highest standards – if it fails, it's back to the drawing-board.

Made Fairly
We are working to ensure that the workers involved in our supply chain – the people that make our books – are treated with fairness and respect.

Responsible Forestry
We are committed to ensuring all our papers come from environmentally and socially responsible forest sources.

For more information, please visit our website at www.egmont.co.uk/ethical

Egmont is passionate about helping to preserve the world's remaining ancient forests. We only use paper from legal and sustainable forest sources, so we know where every single tree comes from that goes into every paper that makes up every book.

This book is made from paper certified by the Forestry Stewardship Council (FSC), an organisation dedicated to promoting responsible management of forest resources. For more information on the FSC, please visit **www.fsc.org**. To learn more about Egmont's sustainable paper policy, please visit **www.egmont.co.uk/ethical**.